MW01028794

Rebecca has a strong desire for women to really know the Word of God in all its depth and richness. She LOVES God's Word and she wants her audience to HUNGER after the TRUTHS that are found there, that those she teaches might come to have a clearer and more beautiful view of God and His attributes.

Rachel Hawkins, Women's Ministry Coordinator

Inspiring! Excellent dramatic monologues. These monologues have been a great blessing to those in our congregation and community. Rebecca's love for God and His Word is evident.

Pastor Dan Kennedy, Brinnon Community Church

One of the elders reported that his daughter-in-law was so touched by your presentation that she went home and reread the story herself! I had the same feeling. I loved how you wove historical facts into it. Other details, as well, added greatly to my enjoyment, as they shed new light on an old beloved story!

Jami Pragnell, Women's Ministry Leader

GOD
means it for
good

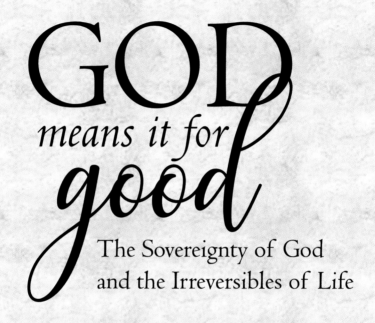

GOD
means it for
good

The Sovereignty of God
and the Irreversibles of Life

Three Biblical stories retold by
Rebecca P. Small

Illustrated by
Diana Elena Neagoe

A publication of Family Reclamation Project

DEDICATION

To all those who have experienced
the fires of persecution or trials
that seem too intense to bear,
the dark valleys of grief
that leave us stunned and numb,
and the deep wounds of offense
that come from difficult relationships.

Apart from such things,
I would never have been in a position
to learn these truths for which I am eternally grateful.

To Dottie Bingham,
whose Bible study taught me the depth of Romans 8:28
and who helped lead me to the comforting reality
of the sovereignty of God.

And to the God
who promises to work all things together
for the good of those who love Him—even the hard things.

CONTENTS

FOREWORD

Have you experienced life-altering "unexpected" events in your earthly journey?

In her book, *God Means It for Good*, Rebecca Small has creatively focused on three women who faced "unexpected" events, telling their unique stories:

- Naomi, an embittered widow, with a Moabite daughter-in-law who insisted on returning with her to Israel.

- A youthful, Babylonian harpist, eyewitness to the fate of three God-fearing men who refused to submit to idolatry.

- Asenath, the daughter of an Egyptian priest, given in marriage to a Hebrew slave who was catapulted into the second highest position in her country.

You will enjoy the fresh perspective of these well-known Bible narratives crafted into first-person monologues. Rebecca's love for

God and delight in studying His Word, meshed with her masterful gift of storytelling, plunges you, the reader, into the historical culture and unique circumstances surrounding three women facing dynamic crossroads. As a reader ask yourself: "Given these unexpected events, how will these women respond? Would I do the same?"

Rebecca and her husband Dan, along with their two teenage daughters, the youngest of seven children, moved into our area in December of 2012 to work with a Christian ministry nearby for the purpose of developing "family-building" events. They attended the church my husband is pastoring. As we developed a friendship with the Smalls, we readily identified with their full-time Christian ministry lifestyle. Hearing stories of Dan's leadership in Christian camping and church ministries as well as his building and contracting skills, along with Rebecca's creative administrative and music (vocal and harp) skills, gave us insight into the motivation behind their service as Bible teachers and writers.

We appreciated the genuineness of Dan and Rebecca sharing their blend of joys, sorrows, and challenges through life's journey. When we first met them, they had just passed through the deep waters of an overarching family sorrow only months before. Their oldest son, Jeremiah (age 33), had been teaching for six years in a private English-speaking school in the Kurdish region of northern Iraq. Shockingly, after routinely opening his class in prayer, he was shot and killed with a handgun by one of his students who then killed himself. This made headline news worldwide. The family was propelled into coping with multiple interviews while participating in several memorial services (Iraq, Tennessee, Washington, Alaska), always using every opportunity to affirm God's forgiveness and their trust in Him. We felt our church needed to hear their story, so my husband asked them to share on a specific Sunday, not realizing it was exactly the one-year anniversary after the tragic death of their son. The Smalls led the church through a very impactful Commemorative Service, dressed in Kurdish traditional style and sharing typical dishes of food from Kurdistan.

Just four months later in July 2013, Rebecca's husband Dan was diagnosed with an incurable, rare bone marrow disease—the "unexpected" again. Our church family had the privilege of praying for, observing, and supporting the Smalls as they trusted God's hand over their husband/father's life. Their ongoing living example strengthened our own faith. We were eyewitnesses of the extreme up-and-down process Dan experienced. Throughout the next two years, he chose to blog, sharing his "way Home to wholeheartedness." He focused intently on Bible truth to sustain his journey, part of which is compiled in the book, *The Jesus Trilogy*. On May 8, 2015, God received this faithful servant.

As Rebecca processed her personal grieving, she began to rewrite and edit these three Biblical narratives, which she had written years earlier, finding her unexpected refining fires now resonating with fresh depth and personal expression in the telling. Having known Rebecca for six years, I can attest this book reflects her own faith declaring, "God Means It for Good!" Rebecca has performed for us all three monologues, dressed in historical costume—two for the whole church and one for our ladies' winter event. We were moved, hearing her personify historical, unexpected, life-altering events that accomplished God's greater Kingdom purposes. Naomi, King Nebuchadnezzar's kingdom, and Joseph's wife were each surprised by purposes greater than any can comprehend!

Now her book is in your hands! Will you open your heart to keep trusting God to faithfully work His good through your own life's unique unexpected journey? His surprise awaits!

Chris Kennedy
Village Missions Pastor's Wife
Brinnon, Washington

ACKNOWLEDGMENTS

My first and highest praise is given to the Holy Spirit. Jesus told His disciples that when He ascended to heaven, He would send the Holy Spirit who would teach us all things and lead us into all truth and righteousness. He has proven Himself to me time and again to be faithful to these promises of Christ. Through the unfolding ages of eternity, I will never cease to be grateful for His faithful ministry to me.

To my daughter, Tirzah, I am constantly amazed at your skills. Thank you for your eye for detail, your patience and endurance in formatting, and your desire for excellence.

To my daughter, Sharon, thank you for all the hours put into finding an illustrator and working with her till the finished product was as we envisioned. Thank you, too, for all the ways you keep our household running and organized.

To Jan Lehmann, I could never thank you enough for the hours and hours you spent with me on the phone going over the final draft.

To Cindy Converse, I am so grateful for your expertise and the hours you gave to help finalize the text. Though our tug-of-war over semicolons may continue, you have taught me much—and I am much more careful and judicious in my use of them!

To Maria Reynolds, your sketches for the story breaks have added the perfect touch. Thank you so much for your quick response and sensitivity to our deadlines. I am so grateful for your friendship and your artistic skills.

To my sister, Lois Bratkovich, I am more than blessed by your faithful love, prayers, and encouragement.

To my church family in Brinnon, Washington, your encouragement has meant more than you'll ever know. You have been the wind in my sails.

To the church family in Yakima, Washington, without your support I could never have done this nor been free to pursue the publishing and performance of these monologues. I pray that your faith and investment in me will bear much fruit for the Kingdom of Christ.

To the Family Reclamation Project board, thank you for believing in this project and letting me run with it.

There are many others who have lifted me up before the Throne of Grace—too many to mention. I am forever humbled and amazed when a friend tells me they have been praying for me—sometimes daily. Eternity alone will tell the true and full story of your impact. I am convinced that I have the best friends in the entire world.

To Eugene Peterson, thank you for your belief in God's use of story and in the Holy Spirit's ability to teach us deeper truth as we put ourselves into the story and use our sanctified imaginations. Your words have encouraged me in this endeavor and articulated my own conviction in approaching the Word of God. I had hoped to put this in your hands personally; now you'll have to observe from the other side of the veil. But your legacy and impact continues.

RPS

Preface

Originally these imaginative biographical sketches were written to be performed as dramatic monologues. I have found that through drama, truth can much more easily be absorbed. People enter into the story and see themselves there. They hear it more clearly and interact with it more fully, perhaps because it is being conveyed in a new and unique way or from a more personal angle. Invariably after each presentation, someone would ask if I had a copy of the narrative in printed form. Eventually it was suggested that I put several of them into a book collection. Here is the first of what I trust will become a series.

The three stories included in the book all have a similar theme. This theme is most precious to my heart; that is, the sovereignty of God is the answer to the troubling circumstances of life. Whether our life journey includes wrongs suffered from evil perpetrated against us, the deaths of those we cherish, persecution for standing on our convictions, trials brought on by natural disasters, or all of the above, the sovereignty of God stands as a strong tower of refuge for us, "the best and safest resting place for our souls," as is stated in one of the stories.

Through my own life's "irreversibles," God has taught me these things. He has used these exact Biblical accounts to give rest and peace to my soul in ways that no earthly counsel could. I have written these stories in an attempt to convey what the Holy Spirit has taught me through His Word, illuminating my understanding as only He can. In many ways, these stories have become my own story. They are the expression of what God has worked into my own soul.

In whatever troubling circumstances you may be facing now or in some future day, dear reader, I pray that these Biblical stories told as first-person experiences will be used by God to minister to your mind and heart. I pray that the sovereignty of God will become your highest and best treasure, as well as the resting place for your soul.

EMBRACE THE

Adapted from Daniel 1-3

INTRODUCTION TO "EMBRACE THE FIRE"

I will never forget the morning I opened my Bible to Daniel 3. The setting is as clear in my mind as if it had been yesterday or I'd had a photo of it. It's been more than thirty years ago now since that day. My husband and I, with three little children, were in the Philippines on a mission assignment. We were young, and I'd never experienced such direct onslaught from the enemy of our souls. My heart was wounded, and I was spiritually drowning. I desperately needed the comfort and ministry of God. No human platitudes would do. I knew the Word of God fairly well, but I needed the Holy Spirit to speak to me for this particular circumstance.

I'd gotten up early to spend time with God in the Bible, praying for Him to speak to me. I opened to where I'd left off the day before: Daniel 3. My eyes caught the italicized paragraph subtitle and I confess, my soul sighed, disheartened. I knew this story well—doesn't everyone who grew up in Sunday school?—the three men in the fiery furnace. I doubted I would get anything out of this familiar chapter and figured this would be a dutiful, rote morning reading.

With that initial thought, I immediately sensed the Holy Spirit's gentle rebuke within. There were no words, but this thought was crystal clear: "Is My Word not deep and unfathomable?" Right then I repented and, agreeing with this inner prompting, lifted my heart in prayer, "Yes, Lord, Your Word is boundless and able to meet my every need." And I asked Him to please teach me.

I don't know that I've ever had such a pointed and astonishing revelation as I had that morning. It could not have been clearer had someone taken a highlighter to my Bible. As I read through the chapter, these words jumped off the page: *bind, bound, bound, bound, unbound.* Well, I won't say more or that would give away the whole story! But, oh, how I pray that as you read, God will reveal to your heart what He revealed to mine that day.

The truths the Holy Spirit taught me those many years ago gave me a completely different perspective on the distressing, weighty trials we were facing at that time. I wanted to find a way to share these truths that had been so remarkably life changing for me. I wanted people to see and feel the dynamics of the story, to put themselves into the scene as eyewitnesses. But how? During my college days, I had been able to fulfill a little-girl dream of mine: learning to play the harp. Four times the text lists the instruments played at this Babylonian event, a harp being one of them. And so was born the idea of telling this all-too-familiar story in a first-person dramatic way through the eyes of the harpist in King Nebuchadnezzar's orchestra.

A few years later the Lord again used this story to bring comfort and reassurance to my soul when I was in the midst of another deeper and much more severe trial. But well over another decade would pass before I was asked to present this monologue. In those intervening years our family went through a series of trials that left us rather shell-shocked. As I began to read through the monologue, preparing for the presentation, I wondered if the truths I'd written about would resonate with me in the same way. Would the things I had learned those years ago still captivate my soul, given my new set of circumstances? Or would they seem trite and shallow? At the end of the reading, with tears streaming down my face, I found myself worshiping the sovereign God of heaven whose unchanging truth had refreshed and stabilized my soul. Once again, the timeless lessons embedded in this historic, Biblical story proved to be an unshakable foundation—one to which we can anchor our souls no matter what storms are hurled at us.

In returning to the story over and over during times of severe trial, I've found that the well of truth has indeed been deep and unfathomable. Each time I think I've surely gotten from it all that could be learned, the Holy Spirit opens a new dimension. Far from becoming old and dim, these truths have become for me, as written in the story, "more precious and more vivid with each passing year." I pray that you also would find comfort and a sure foundation for whatever trials you may encounter and that the "fires" of your life will no longer cause fear but will become treasures to embrace.

EMBRACE THE FIRE

I was there. I saw them. I saw . . . Him. And I understood. To this day I cannot speak of it without becoming completely overwhelmed—more than that—awestruck all over again. I continually ponder, reliving that scene, trying to grapple with all the truths encapsulated there. Though it occurred years ago, I still can picture it as if it were happening before my eyes at this very moment.

I was only a girl at the time, just coming into the blossom of womanhood. I lived in a glorious, golden age. The gods had smiled upon me, favoring me with the good fortune of a pure Babylonian bloodline and parents of high aristocratic status. As I grew up, the empire into which I was born grew vaster and more powerful with each passing year. No nation had been able to withstand King Nebuchadnezzar's army; wealth and slave labor poured into our capital city. Nebuchadnezzar used all this to great advantage, promoting both national and personal aggrandizement.

He was forever coming up with spectacular building projects. He had ordered a massive wall constructed around our entire city as fortification against any invasion. Now this was no ordinary city wall but a double wall, soaring a hundred feet and more into the sky. Over two hundred battle towers rose at intervals along both outer and inner walls, in which skilled archers kept watch throughout night and day. The inner wall was more than thirty feet thick. The chariots of the watchmen could ride atop the wall, somewhat like cars on your modern-day freeways. Oh, how I thrilled to watch those charioteers as they raced, four, five, sometimes six abreast, along the top of the wall around the city!

Eight entryways gave access through the wall into the city. These archways, overlaid in blue marble edged with gold, framed huge bronze doors sculpted in bold relief with lions, the symbol of Nebuchadnezzar's kingdom. They gleamed and sparkled in the sunlight, reflecting their grandeur in the surrounding moat.

Moat? Out in the middle of the desert? Yes! Encircling not just a castle as in your fairy tales, but encompassing our entire city. These waterways, fed by canals from the Euphrates River, facilitated trade around the city as well as provided a further barrier against invasion. Drawbridges, which could be quickly dismantled during threat of war, spanned the moat at every city entrance. On the east side of the city, a third wall had been erected and an additional moat beyond that, as extra protection against the rising strength of the Chaldeans. Nebuchadnezzar did not believe in running risks with fate.

Mere words are insufficient to describe all the other buildings of grandeur King Nebuchadnezzar designed and ordered into existence. Your eyes have never seen anything like it. Resplendent palaces, which furnished residence for the king and his troops, were embellished with flooring of intricate mosaics designed from colorful glazed tile. The inner palace walls of imported wood were draped with the finest brocade tapestries. The magnificent temple to our gods boasted a huge inner chamber overlaid entirely with gold and studded with precious gems, riches our army had plundered from the temples of the impotent gods of other nations. The ancient ziggurat of Nimrod's mighty Babel was restored, reclaiming the hub of the first world power.

And then, of course, there was the unparalleled wonder of the hanging gardens, which the king had built to placate his wife, who sorely missed the lush verdure of her native Africa. A veritable mountain of greenery rose out of a sea of brown barrenness. These terraced gardens were supported with gracefully ornamented pillars upholding the most exotic of plants and tastefully set with bubbling fountains and elegant statues. Ah! If only you could have seen it! Not one to be outdone, Nebuchadnezzar had borrowed his ideas—with much elaboration—from the gardens of Sennacherib, the once mighty king of Assyria.

From my earliest childhood memories, I can recall my parents taking me on walks through the city, telling and retelling me every detail of our glorious history. I never tired of hearing how our great king had governed the construction of each magnificent edifice. We were quite proud of all his accomplishments, for they were symbols of our Babylonian heritage dating back nearly to the beginning of time itself.

Nebuchadnezzar had only to speak the word and it was done. Everyone jumped at his commands. You would, too, if you knew your head would roll—or worse. What few convictions a person may have are held quite lightly in that type of political climate. What's really important is very carefully weighed. One could not afford to hold convictions contrary to those of the king. In fact, it was far better not to have any convictions at all! The only conviction my family held was the firm belief that we should "Obey the king. O King, live forever!" Or during his moments of rage it became, "Appease the king. O King, live . . . forever?"

My family prized security, prestige, and respectable standing above everything. That meant staying on the good side of the king, which wasn't always easy! Even his most trusted advisors weren't safe from his cruel whims. Just prior to the incident I am about to relate to you, he had demanded of his advisors an impossible task. When they, in their shock and disbelief, had been unable to perform it, he had issued a proclamation for all the wise counselors in his entire empire to be executed and their houses torn down till nothing but rubble would be left.

As you can imagine, this was most sobering to us. The whole tone of our family changed after that incident. We became wary and watchful. If his own advisors weren't safe, who was? Mother and Father's faces became lined with worry and fear, a distinct contrast from the confident, proud demeanor of those rising in influence, which they had customarily displayed.

Shortly after that shocking command against his own advisors (which, to the great and astonishing relief of us all, was miraculously averted), we got wind of a new project the king had begun. Now, this was nothing unusual! But our recent fears made us wonder where this one would lead. We'd heard whisperings of an underlying scheme behind all this: a manipulative grasp for more power.

Over the past several months, there had been a growing undercurrent of hostility against the Jews, one of the conquered peoples our army had brought back in bondage and humiliation to our capital city. We did this with all the kingdoms we were victorious over. In this way they would mix with the peoples of other nationalities, thus losing their own national identity. This, in turn, further strengthened our world domination.

But these Jews were different. They refused to intermingle. They maintained a focus we couldn't comprehend and retained the worship of a god we knew nothing about—except that he'd not been powerful enough to deliver them from the mighty arm of King Nebuchadnezzar's army! Though a conquered people, the Jews had been unconquerable in spirit. This was causing a rising tide of suspicion and hatred toward them, which fomented into an almost frenzied, terrorizing desire to crush them. I'd not given much thought to this political undertow.

It was, in fact, one of a small group of Jews who had saved all the king's advisors from being slain. But rather than being grateful, the advisors had resented the favor bestowed upon this singular Jew. Their begrudging attitude, engendered by his ability to do what they had told the king was impossible to do, infected their feelings toward all the Jews and was a response to a particular, unusual event.

Nebuchadnezzar had had a troubling dream, and he couldn't figure out what it meant. But he was unwilling to tell anyone his dream for fear they'd give him some fabricated and fraudulent interpretation. So he mandated that his advisors would first have to relay back to him the dream and then tell its meaning.

Nothing so ridiculously improbable or obviously supernatural had ever been required of any kingly advisor before. Did he expect them to be able to read his mind and to navigate the strange twists and turns our thoughts can take while sleeping? But his decision was firm: tell the dream and its meaning, or die. Only a Hebrew from the conquered land of Israel had been able to do it. The man claimed his god had made known to him both the dream and its interpretation in a night vision as he and a few of his fellow Jews had been praying.

This foreigner had revealed that the king had seen in his dream a great statue, comprised of various precious metals symbolizing successive future world empires. The statue's head, which was of gold, represented none other than our magnificent king, with kingdoms

of lesser power and grandeur following after. Then, a rock hurtling out of heaven smashed the statue and annihilated all other kingdoms, while the rock itself became a great kingdom encompassing the whole earth and lasting forever. Interpreting the past is one thing, but foretelling the future of the world as though it were history? Well, that is quite another! How could a young, foreign captive know these things?

Having interpreted the dream, this Jew went on to advocate for the lives of all the king's advisors. An exceptionally wise man who was also kind and thoughtful? Unheard of! However, the other counselors had been none too thrilled at the gifts and promotion the king had lavished upon this despised outsider. Word had even gotten around that our exalted king—who bowed to no one—had fallen on his face prostrate in worship before this . . . this captive slave. Humph. That might have been rather overdone, don't you think?

But it hadn't stopped there. Nebuchadnezzar went on to appoint this displaced alien as the chief administrator over all the officials and advisors throughout the entire kingdom of Babylon. As a result, they detested this Jewish foreigner. Sheer jealousy! I didn't know what to make of him, but I thought he should be their hero. After all, they owed their very lives to him. But instead, they felt he'd humiliated them. This seemed truly absurd to me. So in my girlish mind, I'd imagined myself impudently saying to them, "Just get over it, O wise ones." And I'd not given it a second thought. But politics is . . . politics. They didn't get over it. Their resentment had only deepened with time.

In the midst of this political climate, I was summoned for orchestra duty. Nebuchadnezzar reveled in pomp and ceremony; every event of his was a grandiose extravaganza. For this and other reasons, my parents had worked hard to secure for me an upfront position in the king's orchestra. But considering recent events, they suddenly realized that my life could easily be in danger. They feared for me to stay in the orchestra, but they feared just as much to pull me out. With great reluctance they let me go that day. So I stayed on as one of the harpists in King Nebuchadnezzar's orchestra.

On the appointed day we were to report to the plain of Dura, a large, isolated fortification out in the middle of the barren desert. As we neared the plain, we caught sight of this colossal statue towering far above the high stone wall surrounding the military training ground. It was an astounding ninety feet to the top of the crown, and the chest had a depth of nine feet. The exact features of King Nebuchadnezzar. Solid gold. It was absolutely stunning! We stood gaping up at it for long minutes, hushed and awestruck, until the sun, glinting off it, forced us to turn our eyes away.

So this was the new building project! That dream had certainly gone to his head, as evidenced by this imposing gold replica of himself. It appeared Nebuchadnezzar was attempting to rewrite the future, with his kingdom swallowing up all the others and becoming the one that would stand undestroyed forever. I'd always known the king was utterly egotistical, but I had excused it. He deserved to be. After all, he was the greatest king in all of known history! But this? Even I thought he had gone a bit too far.

As I tuned my harp, it became rather comical to watch others as they arrived at the scene. Without fail, all faces surveyed the height of that prodigious statue with an initial transfixed upward look of jaw-dropping wonder. And then, as I had done, they each began to furtively look around. What was all this about?

Directly behind the statue was a lofty platform with an impressively ornate and massive throne for the king, flanked on either side with chairs of lesser note for his highest officials. To the right of the king's platform was a broader and slightly lower level for the orchestra; and to the left, some little distance away, was a large stone furnace already burning.

The day had begun typically—hot and sultry. The furnace was not needed for warmth. What was its purpose? Neighboring kingdoms to the east sometimes built stone furnaces along the roadsides for political executions. It was this gruesome reality that filled our hearts with suspicion and dread, and I could feel the grip of fear slowly fastening its hold upon me.

All the leaders throughout all the provinces of Babylon had been assembled by royal decree. There were representatives from every known and conquered language and nationality. Having transferred their loyalty, for political and personal expediency, to their newly adopted king, these "heads of state" were now playing the roles of tribute collectors and petty court judges administering Babylonian law over their own people. Anybody who was anybody in the entire empire was there.

Presently, in a mighty fanfare, the great King Nebuchadnezzar ascended to his throne. Then a herald stepped to the platform.

That vast sea of dignitaries stood in silent uneasiness, awaiting the king's latest whim. In a strong booming voice that echoed over the surrounding plain, the herald shouted out, "This is what you are commanded to do, O peoples, nations, and men of every language . . ." He went on to proclaim that as soon as they heard the sound of the horn, flute, zither, lyre, harp, pipes, and all kinds of music, they were to fall down and worship the image of gold, which King Nebuchadnezzar had set up.

Then followed the political threat: Whoever did not fall down and worship would be cast immediately into the blazing furnace. At that

last pronouncement I involuntarily sucked in my breath. My heart started racing and my skin began to crawl. So that was the purpose for the furnace: a human oven. And I had to play for THIS?! Inwardly I prayed frantically to the gods, *Please, please don't let anyone remain standing!* I could not let myself think of the horror of it.

My hands were clammy and shaking. How ... could I ... play? The others around me were preparing to play; they appeared to be having no problem. Was their personal fear preventing them from showing any signs of disagreement? Or had their hearts become cold and hard like the king's statue? Yes! Yes, that's what the statue symbolized: not awe, not grandeur, but a cold, hard, wicked heart. With that thought, my mind and heart recoiled from the gargantuan monstrosity.

We were given the signal. With our first note, that vast assemblage flattened themselves in the dust. I felt disdain and shame. We were a nation of cowardly puppets dancing on the strings of our sovereign's arrogant cruelty. I didn't want to be one of them, yet I was one of them. My own heart, too, shrank in fear—of death—and I knew I would have fallen down with all the rest. We continued to play while they continued to grovel. No one dared so much as rear up his head.

My nerves were beginning to relax as a sense of relief settled over me. That nightmarish threat didn't need to be carried out. But then, out of the corner of my eye, I caught sight of some Chaldean officials making their way to the king's platform. We stopped playing. Heads began tenuously lifting to steal a timid glance.

I couldn't catch what the men were saying, but their actions were so sniveling and obsequious. As they spoke, the king's countenance grew darker and darker. I watched with horror-filled eyes as he flew into a mad rage. Leaping to his feet, he thundered, "Bring them to me!"

No! No! No! I'd not seen anyone. My eyes scanned the prostrate crowd. A restless stirring swept over the throng as subtle and furtive as a dry desert wind over the sand. We barely dared to breathe though our hearts were thumping like kettledrums.

From the midst of the crowd, three men were brought forward, wending their way through the cowering bodies. As they came closer, I lowered my head into my hands—Jews. I might have known. I could tell by their clothing and the cut of their features. They were Jews. This was nothing more than a political vendetta. My horror began to meld into anger.

I was angry at those Chaldeans . . . and I was angry with these three Jews. Why didn't they bow? Was that such a hard thing to do? Were they such recent captives to Babylon? Didn't they know about our king? Or were they just too proud of their national heritage? "You fools!" I wanted to shout at them.

My eyes darted back and forth between King Nebuchadnezzar and the approaching three. The king's anger settled into a malicious, eager pleasure. Ah, yes! This was just the kind of power play he relished. It seemed an eternity before they finally stood before him.

Nebuchadnezzar spoke like a serpent, excessively condescending. "Is it true, Shadrach? Meshach? Abednego?" He addressed them individually by name, looking at each one in turn. How did he know who they were? Could it be possible that these were of that small group of Jews who had helped save all the advisors from execution? "Is it true that you do not serve my gods nor worship the image of gold I have set up?" He gave them no time to answer.

"Now, when you hear the sound of the horn, flute, zither, lyre, harp, pipes, and all kinds of music," he glanced toward the orchestra, "if you are ready to fall down and worship the image of gold I have made," he paused, narrowing his eyes, "very good."

How benevolent, I thought with sarcasm. But at least he was giving them a second chance. He wasn't having them thrown in "immediately" as the herald had proclaimed. Perhaps Nebuchadnezzar really didn't want to kill these particular men.

At that point, the king's voice began to rise, anger flickering in his eyes as he continued. "But if you do not worship it," and at this he rose to his feet. Imposing his full height upon them, he thrust his arm toward the furnace, "you will be thrown immediately into the blazing fiery furnace!" Then, raising his hands toward heaven with his face leaning into theirs, he cried, "Then what god will be able to save you from my hand?"

Momentarily I closed my eyes and shook my head as a tremor shot up my spine. He was right. Of course, he was right. No gods, including theirs, had been able to save their people from King Nebuchadnezzar's hand. I was all too ready to play this time. I tilted my harp back in preparation. Fastening my eyes on the conductor, I awaited the signal. *Let's play. Let's play!* was screaming in my head. Surely they would bow.

But no signal came. One of the three men began to speak. His calm, clear, respectful tone captured my attention. My eyes were drawn to him in amazement, and I set my harp upright for a better view. They were not backing down or trembling with fright as I was. They stood erect and dignified, without cowardice or shame. "O Nebuchadnezzar, we do not need to defend ourselves before you in this matter."

What? Didn't need to defend themselves? Why, that's all I'd ever known—people blubbering and defending themselves before the king. It was a way of life. So, apparently the king did know of their loyal service.

My thoughts were interrupted—what was that he was saying? "... the God we serve is able to save us from the blazing fiery furnace, and He will rescue us from your hand, O King."

How could they say that? Their god had not rescued them when Nebuchadnezzar's army had ransacked their land. How could they believe he was powerful enough now to save them from the blazing fire roaring in the furnace (the heat of which they could undoubtedly already feel) and from the unquestioned authority of the very king himself standing right there before them? None of our gods could do this.

However, it was his final statement that really arrested me. "But if not, we want you to know, O King, that we will not serve your gods, nor worship the image of gold you have set up."

Their words sent chills clear through me. "But if not"? It was spoken so deliberately, without any hesitation whatsoever. There was no pause to stop and think about it. Perhaps they had known about this event before it happened and had already determined what they would do. But what exactly did he mean? Was he suggesting the king might decide not to throw them in? Well, it was pretty clear what the king intended to do, and he was not one to change his mind! But life or death, to these young men it didn't matter what the king chose.

"But if not" . . . Or could he mean—my mind was reeling at the possible intent—that even if their god did not rescue them in this final hour? Clearly, they understood that He is God, who does what He pleases. And they were but mere mortal men, destined to die sometime. Most evidently, there was no presumption on their part regarding what this God of theirs was obligated to do, as if He owed them anything. Yet they stood resolute concerning their responsibility toward Him.

Regardless of the king's actions or their God's actions, their loyalty belonged to God and seemed, in fact, due Him. They refused to bow before . . . a lie. Suddenly the truth dawned upon me: the statue and our gods are all lies. They are false gods, who have eyes, but they cannot see. They have ears, but they cannot hear. Mouths they have, but they've never spoken one word. Oh, yes, they have feet, but they've never moved one inch from the place where they've been set. They are only images created by the hand of man. But their God—could it be that He is uncreated and indeed the Truth?

Though these men believed that their God *could* rescue them, they recognized He might *choose* not to. Yet even then He was worthy of their faith, their loyalty, and their worship! What God was this? Here was the embodiment of true conviction, of open-handed integrity. They served God for Himself alone,[1] not for what He might do for them. To them, He was—and is—the only One worthy of bowing before in honor and homage. He alone deserved their greatest and highest gift and treasure: Worship.[2] Suddenly I no longer wanted them to bow down.

But Nebuchadnezzar was so furious at being unable to cause them to crack or even to bend under his fear tactics, that he gave the most insane order ever: "Heat the furnace seven times hotter!" Why? What difference does it make if the fire is hot or hotter? It will kill you either way! Perhaps Nebuchadnezzar was trying to make his fire more consuming than their God—the God who had obviously already consumed these three men. Some servants rushed to stoke the fire.

Then Nebuchadnezzar bawled out another command: "Bind them!" And he specifically chose his mightiest war heroes to come and bind the men. But no great feat of strength or prowess was needed. The three men didn't fight or even struggle but calmly submitted. What amazing trust! I winced as these brawny soldiers, with their muscles rippling, cinched thick ropes around the men's wrists, winding the bonds tightly around their bodies to secure arms, legs, and ankles, rendering them utterly immobile. They didn't remove their cloaks and tunics, or even their turbans! I suppose

---

[1] Timothy Keller, *Walking with God through Pain and Suffering* (London: Penguin Books, 2015), p. 292.
[2] http://srussellfnp.blogspot.com/2017/05/surrender.html.

Nebuchadnezzar must have thought their clothing would add more fuel to his fire and ignite the men more quickly.

The king viewed all this coolly with an evil smirk, but the look in his eyes belied his satisfaction. In conquering, he knew he'd been conquered! The rope binding done, he wildly gestured for these choicest of his fighting men to throw them in. The cruelty of this man—our king, in whom we'd taken such pride—went beyond my comprehension. A most unworthy object for my worship. My awe and admiration of him turned to loathing.

The officials seated on either side of his throne acted so disgustingly diplomatic throughout the whole affair. Looking dead ahead, expressionless, and occasionally nodding their obeisant approval at his every word, they were most willing to sit by and do nothing, for fear of incurring the king's fanatic rage themselves. Oh, how I wished I had the strength to throw in my lot with the Hebrews—just to spite him. But I, too, feared death. How could they do this?

For several moments the air itself seemed to hold its breath. Perspiration ran down people's faces; muscles twitched. We couldn't bear to see, yet we couldn't pull our eyes away. Like stone statues we watched as the three courageous men were hurled into the mighty inferno. Our eyes widened with increased horror as the soldiers who threw them in faltered and, reeling from the fiery blast, themselves fell down dead in twisted contortions. My gaze darted to Nebuchadnezzar. A brief, stunned shudder swept over his face before he regained his nonchalant disdainful look.

I dropped my head and turned away. Surely these three Jews were the best men in the entire kingdom—and they were gone. Tears of both grief and anger welled into my eyes. The injustice, the unbridled power that could cause such wrong! The loss tore and gaped within me. A great emptiness crept over me . . . a hopelessness filled with despair . . . and a blackness as still as death itself. Time stopped.

But, oh! Oh, if I could describe to you what happened next! The gruesome tension that had held us all so infinitely quiet for so long now suddenly shattered. Low gasps and murmurs rippled through the crowd. The king leapt up, getting the attention of his highest officials. His voice was frantic and husky—frightened, most terribly frightened. "Were there not three men whom we bound and threw into the fire?"

The expressionless officials now put on a wise air. Stroking their beards, they said in deep, fawning tones, "True, O King." *Where*

was the "live forever"? flashed sardonically across my mind. They probably didn't really want him to live forever at that moment.

"LOOK!" he fairly screamed at them. I strained forward. I was sure I saw it, too. "I see four men walking around in the fire, unbound and unharmed—and the fourth looks like the son of the gods."

Yes. Yes! I saw Him. I stared in fixed wonder and disbelief. I couldn't take in enough. Who had ever known or seen a living God?

Nebuchadnezzar staggered like a drunken man toward the furnace. Everyone was in such shock; his officials didn't even move to stop him. *He will die like his soldiers,* I gasped inwardly.

But he stopped short and shouted into the glaring mouth of the furnace, "Shadrach, Meshach, Abednego, servants of the Most High God," (Truly, he got that right!) "come out! Come here!" Out the three walked.

My mind began to race. Blinding lightning bolts of revelation flashed upon me in rapid succession. Nebuchadnezzar's thundering "Bind them" still rang in my ears, as did his terror-choked, "Did we not throw three men bound into the fire? But I see four men, unbound!"

In that instant I began to understand truths that have grown more vivid and more precious with each passing year. Bound . . . bound . . . unbound. Do you see? Oh, do you see God's purposes for the fiery trials He allows us to be thrown into? The only things the fire burned were the ropes that bound them. Oh, Consuming Fire, set us free! For if the Son of God shall set you free, you shall be free indeed.

And not just unbound, but four instead of three. The very Son of the living God came into the fire and revealed Himself to them there. Our trials open our eyes to revelations of God we would not otherwise see. They also present us with opportunities for real and intimate experiences of walking with the living God, of knowing Him in ways that deepen and broaden our lives. Could there be anything more valuable than this? To walk with Him, to know Him—whom to know, I was now convinced, is life eternal.

Later I learned from the ancient Jewish scrolls that a man under deep duress, in severe anguish and bodily affliction, had defied his

present realities and declared with absolute certainty, "Though worms destroy this body, yet in my flesh shall I see God, my own eyes, and not another!"[3] He was proclaiming eternal resurrection Life! No wonder these men didn't fear death. For the first time in my life, conviction began to take root and grow in my heart. I wanted a faith like theirs. No—much more than that—I wanted a God like theirs.

Not one hair was singed. Their clothes were completely intact. They didn't even smell like smoke. All decorum and fear were abandoned as the provincial leaders pressed in around them to see—to touch—men over whom fire had no power. I used to think that when someone went through a deep and fierce trial, it would mark them for the rest of their lives, etching itself into the very fabric of their facial features. Now I know differently. If we walk through it with the Son of the living God, our souls will be fully protected. There will not be one shred of evidence, not even the smell of smoke—no matter how multiplied the heat of the fire. The only marks: freedom and the radiance of the Son of God upon our countenance.

Amid the pandemonium and before that vast array of provincial leaders, our king now openly blessed the God of Shadrach, Meshach, and Abednego. But one sentence the king said in this concluding speech emblazoned its words upon my heart: "They trusted in Him and defied the king's command, yielding their bodies rather than serve or worship any god except their own God."

A God worthy of trust regardless of the outcome? Yes. Yes! A thousand times, *yes!* No god but theirs is worthy of such worship,

---

[3] Job 19:26-27.

such unfeigned loyalty. They yielded their bodies only to God—even to death. In spirit, in soul, and in body they were consumed with God.

It was not their courage that saved them; it was their God—the living God, Creator of all, Sustainer of all, who is above all and has power over all. He was their total fixation. Nothing else mattered: neither life nor death, nor principalities nor powers. In the end it was safer to be on the side of their God all the way around, whether the king was for you or against you. Kings rise and fall as does their favor. But God remains the same, forever faithful to His own.

In an effort to regain control, our volatile king now announced this threatening decree: Anyone—any people, nation, or language—would be slashed in pieces and their houses burned into a heap of ashes if they dared so much as to speak even one word against the God of Shadrach, Meshach, and Abednego. And he added, "For there is no other god who can deliver like this."

The testimony of these three ordinary men who had an extra-ordinary God impacted an entire world empire, shifting the focus of the king and all those within his realm to the true and living God. Even though the personal life experience of these men had appeared to be, on the human level, a long journey of successive defeats, it was, in truth, the pathway to a great and most glorious victory! God, not Nebuchadnezzar and not his army, had brought them to Babylon. Oh! Even now I'm beginning to see . . . The presence of these Jews was not just for King Nebuchadnezzar and the empire of Babylon. God brought them for me.

I have found freedom and the knowledge of the Son of God through them. Their testimony, their faith, their God have consumed me. And now, perhaps through my story, you might find . . . Ah! What a humbling and awesome thought! I wonder, who might be touched through your experience with the living God?

You know, after all was said and done, the king promoted them. Even this bore a truth. The promotion given by the king was merely temporal, but there is a reward far beyond the things of this life that had captured the vision and the hearts of these men. If we, like them, persevere, determined to endure with our eyes fixed on the true and living God, we will never be disappointed. On the other side of our trials, innumerable blessings await us. As one of the great Hebrew kings has written of God: "At Your right hand are pleasures forevermore."[4] They knew that. They staked their lives on that.

The things I learned that day burn like a blazing fire within me, increasingly hotter and hotter. Freedom. The revelation and presence of the Son of God. Eternal resurrection Life. No evidence of fire. Turning others to the true and living God. Pleasures forevermore. I KNOW. I was there. I saw.

If the fire yields such incalculable treasures as these, should we not embrace it? Yes! Blessed Fire.

---
[4] Psalm 16:11.

From Bitter to Blessed

Adapted from Ruth 1-4

Introduction to
From Bitter to Blessed

More than once when I have performed this monologue, someone has asked me afterwards if I felt like this was my own story. Well, yes, and no. I have never experienced the fear, the uncertainty, the devastation of famine as Naomi did and as many others around the world and down through history have. I have not lost all my immediate family members. The trauma and void created by such loss is impossible to adequately even imagine.

Yet I have experienced the irreversible losses of death: the shocking soul ravages of a sudden loss and the hope-consuming deterioration of a slow loss. Our oldest son was a high school teacher in northern Iraq. He loved his job and went back to it with increasing anticipation year after year—until he was shot one day in his classroom by one of his students. None of us will ever forget that frozen-in-time moment when we learned of this tragedy. It is forever etched upon our hearts and minds. Just over a year later, my husband was diagnosed with a terminal illness. For two years he battled the roller coaster of that disease before breathing his last on this earth.

I first started studying the book of Ruth years ago before either of those losses. As a nine-year-old child, I had experienced the sudden death of my father. Loss and sorrow became familiar to me early in life. But when I took a group of women through the study of Ruth, I was in a different season with a growing family. However, since loss had marked me at a young age, I could in some measure enter into the feelings of the book.

As I studied, I came to see that the book of Ruth is not so much about Ruth as it is about Naomi. Each of the four chapters in this concise little book ends with a comment about or by Naomi, leading us with raw honesty through the phases of growth in her relationship with God. The book chronicles the journey of her life, and through her story we are given a very vivid illustration of the sovereignty of God, unveiling the ways God uses loss in the lives of His people for His good and wise purposes.

From that study I wrote this monologue. At that point in my life, I could look back on the major loss of my earlier childhood and trace the hand of God leading our family through the grief and beyond to a wonderful redemptive end. I never tire of telling the story of my own mother's faith that, when put to new tests as a widow, clearly proved the faithfulness of God in our lives.

It wasn't until my more recent losses that I returned to my earlier writing of this story. I expanded it some, having learned more. But basically the message and writing remained the same. The book of Ruth poignantly portrays one woman's passage through the stages of grief. Beyond all doubt, this seemingly simple love story displays the understanding of God into the depth and breadth of our sorrows.

One day, while I was practicing for a presentation of this monologue, a realization came to me: I had bypassed the struggle with bitterness because of Naomi. She had been my mentor those years ago, teaching me such valuable truths about God's sovereignty that my soul was anchored during my own times of catastrophic loss.

I pray that the overarching wisdom reflected in God's sovereignty will become an anchor for your own soul.

From Bitter to Blessed

Were it not for my daughter-in-law, my story would be buried along with countless others who have suffered down through history. Oh, what a precious gift she has been. God taught me so much about Himself through her. Let me see if I can recount these things to you. First, I learned that God—oh dear, I am forever running off ahead of myself. Giving you a list will never help you understand all I've learned! Truth is discovered in the journey of life. It is the story God marks out for us that reveals His truth to our hearts. I must digress and tell you the whole of it, so that perhaps—oh, how I pray—you might catch even a small glimpse of the hope you have, because of who your God is.

I lived during a painful and shameful time of Israel's history. We had been given great privilege: God had displaced other cultures and peoples because of their grievous sins, giving us their land to make a new life for ourselves. After bringing us out of slavery in Egypt, God had repeatedly warned us to stay far away from the abominable practices of the surrounding nations, for those practices led to much heartache and depravity. We, who had the heritage of which no other nation on earth could boast, had ourselves turned from the God who had worked so mightily on our behalf to rescue us from cruel bondage. He had favored us with this good and pleasant land, yet we chose the very evils He had warned against.

Joshua had led us in victory into this Promised Land and had exhorted us time and again to walk in the ways of Yahweh, the one true God who had revealed Himself to Moses. We were to keep His commandments faithfully and teach them diligently to our children. But Joshua and all those who had witnessed firsthand the awesome miracles of God had long been dead. And our people forgot. Few followed the ways of Yahweh any longer, and fewer still passed on His truth to their children.

Because of our disobedience as a nation, we had gone through one cycle of oppression after another. The strain and burden of foreign domination would at last cause our people to cry out to Yahweh for deliverance. Seeking Yahweh's aid necessarily led to studying the holy manuscripts written down by Moses and Joshua. Through them we saw the vast breach of our guilt—all the ways we had disobeyed the word of Yahweh and dishonored His holy name, His character, and His covenant.

This, in turn, would lead to a wave of repentance and turning from our wickedness. With each turning, Yahweh mercifully raised up a strong leader to push back the enemy powers, thus judging our oppressors. Then would follow a time of peace and blessing.

Prosperity would return, and close on its heels crept in our apathy toward Yahweh and His ways. And so the cycle would repeat itself as we descended once again into dark days.

When I was a young woman, how grateful I was both to God and to my parents for choosing a godly man for me to marry: Elimelech. His name stood staunchly against the prevailing culture, in stark contrast to one of the supposed "judges" of our days. After Gideon, one of our God-ordained judges, had led us to an astounding victory over our oppressors, the people wanted to make him their king. But he had refused, saying, "Neither I nor my sons shall rule over you. The Lord shall rule over you." But later, he had named one of his sons Abimelech, meaning, "My father is king." This man, reckless, harsh, and self-serving, had appointed himself as one of our judges.

My husband's name proclaimed a different message: "My God Is King." Elimelech never doubted the sovereign control of Yahweh; his soul found rest in that truth. How I loved Elimelech for this! I found solace in the strength of his faith and in his confidence in the Lord.

Not long after we were married, God blessed us with a son. In those days we chose names for our children that reflected something about their lives. We were again under oppression; we were suffering. Our son was sickly from the day he was born. We named him Mahlon, which means sickly and suffering.

I'll never forget the night my dear husband came through the door of our home after a town meeting, his face haggard and worn, his shoulders sagging because God's laws were being cast aside as irrelevant. Everyone did what was right in his or her own eyes. The Word of the Lord was considered outdated and wholly unfit to speak to the issues of our day and our culture. "Times have changed," they said. Right and wrong were based on current opinion and public consensus—as if God needed our vote of approval!

Month by month we had seen the good hand of God's blessing being lifted from our land. All the curses God had warned about through His servant Moses fell upon us once again. Israel became the tail and not the head. The Midianites from the east swooped down upon us and plundered our fields just as we were preparing to harvest. In no time at all, we were reduced to extreme poverty. In a strange paradoxical twist, Bethlehem, the name of our hometown, which means "the House of Bread," became a place of starvation. There was no food anywhere.

I was afraid—afraid of what would become of us and our children, for by this time I was pregnant with our second child. Though we were thrilled to have another son, Elimelech's face was lined with worry over how he would provide for us. We named our second son Chilion: leanness, for he was so thin and frail that we were afraid he might just fade away and perish. In mercy, God spared the lives of both our sons. They lived to become grown men.

So out of those early uncertain days flowed an ever-widening sense of personal gratitude, even in the midst of a degenerating culture. I'd always had a positive outlook on life, and I sought to put the best face on our circumstances. Though life was indeed hard, I found my roles as both wife and mother most pleasant, as my name indicated.

But Elimelech? Night after night he would sit on a stool by the table and pray, seeking Yahweh. He became so burdened for our nation and our family that his body would rock and sway with distress. Then one night after the two boys had gone to bed, Elimelech sat me down to talk. I'd never seen him with such a hollow, empty look on his face. He said he'd been doing a lot of thinking and praying.

"Yes, I'd seen that," I acknowledged, attempting to comfort him.

For several seconds his eyes searched mine deeply before saying that he felt, until this hard time was over, we needed to move to Moab.

"Moab?! Why Moab?" Indignation immediately arose within me as I cried out, "Cursed be Moab for enticing Israel into immorality and idolatry! We are to have nothing to do with them."

He knew all this. Rather than comforting him, I had only succeeded in adding to his grief. When he looked back up at me, there was no light left in his eyes as he spoke with a dull, measured fierceness, "Naomi, I have to feed my family."

Numb and wordless, we packed what few belongings we could carry with us. Many of my dear friends came to say good-bye. Perhaps my own conflicting inner wrestlings fueled my imagination, but it seemed their countenances bore a mixture of sadness and compassion along with condemnation and veiled disdain—as if somehow we were betraying them by leaving the land promised to our fathers.

As we turned with tear-filled eyes to take one last look back at Bethlehem, Elimelech pulled me toward him and whispered, "Yahweh will be with us even there, Naomi. It won't be long. We'll come back as soon as we're able . . ." His voice trailed off.

The weeks and months in Moab turned into years. Over and over again, I kept reassuring myself, *This is only temporary—just until . . . until . . .* Then suddenly, my husband died. I was plunged into a deep grief that I could not see my way out of. With him were buried all our hopes and dreams of ever returning to Israel and getting back to a normal life.

From Bitter to Blessed

My two sons knew Moab better than they knew Israel. They came of age there. Naturally, they wanted to marry. Elimelech wasn't there to counsel and direct them, and I felt helpless to change their minds. So they married—Moabite women? *O God, how can I accept this? Was this not a strictly forbidden alliance?*

But eventually I too came to love them as my boys did. Here and there, now and then, I tried to share with them about Yahweh. I wanted them to know the one true God of Israel and to see the falseness of their idols. I wanted my grandchildren to grow up knowing Yahweh. But they gave me no grandchildren.

No . . . No! Just as suddenly as my husband had gone, my two sons also died. I was crushed with grief. Why had the Lord not taken me as well? I remember but few things from that time of my life; it is a blur of blackness. I only remember feeling lost, alone, and forsaken. I was confused and frightened. The words of Job from the ancient scrolls, which I had heard from childhood, haunted me: "Naked I came from my mother's womb; naked I shall return from where I came. The Lord gives and the Lord takes away. Blessed be the name of the L—. . ."[1]

I sought to affirm these truths, but I choked on the last word. It would not come out. Noble words, but they were not the echo of my own heart. It seemed each time they replayed in my mind, I became more cynical. Where was God in all this? Had we been wrong to come to Moab? Was this God's judgment on us for mingling with the Moabites? Why? Why had He left me desolate? Why had He left me to provide for two Moabite daughters-in-law? Why? Why?—a thousand *why*'s and ten thousand *if only*'s.

I tried to pray, but I could not. The heavens seemed like brass to me. God was silent. I truly believed God had abandoned me because we had come to Moab, that somehow it was my fault. Perhaps I'd not tried hard enough to convince my husband not to come here? I didn't know.

Then one day in the market, I overheard news from some merchants that the famine in Israel was over. A buried yearning awakened within me. I didn't belong here; these could never be my people. Gradually over the next few days and weeks, a plan began

---

[1] Job 1:21

to form in my mind. It would not and could not ever be the same. But I would go back—back to my home and back to my people.

I told the two girls. As we prepared to leave, I couldn't get away from two gnawing thoughts. I was getting old and could provide neither food nor husbands for them. And, being Moabites, they would not be accepted. There was no future for them in Israel. The girls had been good to me, so kind in our mutual grief, and I would miss them dearly. But it was better for me to go back alone and bear this heavy bitterness on my own.

The day we were to start our journey, I firmly told them to return to their mothers' homes. Then, desperately clinging to the thin thread of my faith, I blessed them with a parting prayer: "May Yahweh deal kindly with you as you have dealt with—" I hesitated, the words catching in my throat, "the dead—and with me."

I also prayed that Yahweh would grant that they might find rest in the homes of new husbands. Rest? I hadn't known rest for so long. Rest for my soul, for my tormented thoughts and tortured emotions. Rest. Our Hebrew word comes from the name of Noah: *menuach*. As Lamech, his father, had expressed when he prophetically named his baby boy, "This one will comfort us, give us rest, from our labor and toil." They too had lived during dark, difficult days. But even through that terrible judgment in his lifetime, Noah had been used by God to provide a refuge of safety and security—and even to bring about renewal. *Menuach:* that's what I desired for my daughters-in-law. This was the God I wanted them to know, even as my own hope for *menuach* faltered.

I kissed them both, and they wept aloud. They wanted to go with me. With all the determination I could muster, I pressed them to turn back, entreating them to return to their own people, to find rest in the homes of new husbands, and to start a new life for themselves. Looking back, I now realize there was a certain smugness of self-pity in my attempts to dissuade them. And I actually said, "No, my daughters; for it grieves me very much for your sakes that the hand of the Lord has gone out against me." For it seemed His judgment was meant only for me. Their grief might pass, but mine would not.

From Bitter to Blessed

You hear (don't you?) how I was blaming God? Yet ultimately, every grief in our lives must necessarily trace back to God, for we know that Yahweh is sovereign over all. The one true God is worthy of our "why's," and He alone is capable of handling them—though He is not obligated to explain Himself. The journey of this life, regardless of the circumstances, is one of learning to trust both the wisdom and the goodness of a sovereign God, even when we cannot see it. But this was the one thing I could not bring myself to do.

They cried some more. But me? No tears would come though I wished they would. My soul was detached, not allowing me to express

the reality of my heart. We hugged one another long and hard. Finally, Orpah turned away.

I tried to tear myself away from Ruth, begging her to please not make this any harder. Then the truth of what we both knew asserted itself as I implored her to go back as Orpah had done, to her own people and her own g-g-gods—? Did I really want that? Did it not matter anymore? It was not just a turning back to their mothers' homes, but a return to a culture of false gods—and all the evils that follow in their wake.

Ruth understood this fully, and she clung to me sobbing, "Entreat me not to leave you, nor to return from following after you. For wherever you are going, I will go; wherever you lodge, I will lodge. Your people will be my people and your God, my God. Where you die, I will die and there I will be buried. The Lord do to me and more also if anything but death parts you and me."

How could I turn her away after that? Ruth claimed my people and my God with such resolve; I had no more words. This dear Moabite woman had come to find shelter and comfort—yes, even rest—in the almighty Yahweh of Israel. She put me to shame. For I found no comfort or rest in God.

For the most part we traveled the fifty miles to Bethlehem in silence. Ruth seemed to understand the churning in my soul, the turmoil of emotions in returning to my hometown.

Bethlehem is a small village, one where we all, for the most part, knew each other. Our departure those ten-plus years ago had been known by all, so my return alone after all these years caused quite a stir. My old friends came to welcome me home. Seeing their faces, their husbands, their grown children, and their grandchildren swept a crushing wave of fresh grief over me.

The bitterness that had been simmering in my soul finally boiled over. I could not bear to hear them call me Naomi, and I spoke with blunt honesty. "Don't call me Naomi! I am not pleasant anymore.

Call me Mara, for I am bitter—bitter at Yahweh." Oh, did I really say that? I suppose, being among friends again, I felt safe at last to unburden my soul.

"He who is the Almighty One of Israel, the One who is more than enough, El Shaddai"—that Name seemed to mock my circumstances, taunting me with questions and doubts. "He has dealt bitterly with me." I recklessly continued on, "He could have prevented all this from happening, but He did not." I felt as if the Lord had taken me to court, witnessed against me, and handed down a harsh sentence upon me.

I'd allowed grief to harden my heart. I lifted my eyes to these dear friends of mine, hoping they could read in them the sorrow of my soul. "I left here full," I lamented, "but the Lord has brought me back empty. Yahweh has afflicted me."

Later when I was alone, I mulled over those last words of mine. How ironic. We left Bethlehem because we had felt so empty and destitute. Now I looked back on those days as being full. *Oh, Elimelech, I had you and Mahlon and Chilion! We had so much! Why*

did we ever leave? Would you all still be alive had we stayed? Now I truly have nothing.

Oh, how my grief had blinded me. Dear Ruth never took offense, hearing me say those words, nor did she wallow in my bitterness. Quietly, subtly, persistently, God kept working in my life, though I did not then have the eyes or the faith to see it.

The barley harvest was just beginning when we arrived, and the crop that year was bountiful with God's blessing. Harvest times are always occasions of hope. And through a young Moabitess, God was reaching out to me to restore my faith and my hope in Him, the all-good, all-wise, all-powerful, true and living God.

Ruth had an insatiable thirst to know God. So as life unfolded, I shared with her all I knew of Him, His ways, and His laws. She saw His love in all His commands and decrees and was especially impressed with His care for the poor. The gods of Moab were not like that. Their favor could be curried only by the very rich who might have the means to give all that the gods demanded.

When Ruth learned of the gleaners' law, she asked if she could please go gather grain for our needs. Far from expecting me to provide for her, Ruth wanted to provide for me. I was humbled by her love and gave her my blessing.

The first day she went out, I was so anxious for her. I worried about the heat from the sweltering Judean sun. I worried about whether she would have enough food and water to sustain herself. But I worried mostly about her safety. There were still so many evil men in Israel who would have no conscience whatsoever about violating a Moabitess. They might even think they were doing God a favor, for the Moabites were under God's curse anyway. All day long, fear clawed at my heart. I pleaded with God to protect her, though I wasn't sure He even heard or answered my prayers anymore.

Oh, I can't tell you the relief that surged through me when I finally saw her coming down the road. I ran out to meet her and helped her carry her load into the house. I was astonished at how much she had gleaned. And, bless her heart, she had already threshed it as well. There was even a small packet of bread and roasted grain.

I peppered her with questions, repeating myself in my eagerness to hear the whole story. "Where did you glean today? Where did you work? How were you able to glean so much? Where did you get this extra food?" And without giving her time to answer, "Blessed be the one who took notice of you."

When I finally paused to take a breath, Ruth simply said, "The man's name in whose field I gleaned was Boaz."

"Boaz? Boaz! May he be blessed of the Lord!" Suddenly the truth began to dawn upon me: "The Lord has not forsaken His kindness to the living—or to the dead." Boaz was not only a godly man, and a wealthy one, but he was also a close relative of my husband. "Why, he is a kinsman-redeemer to us!" I exclaimed.

Ruth looked puzzled, so I explained, "According to the Law of God, if a woman's husband dies, leaving no children, a near relative may marry the widow so that she might bear children for the deceased. In this way his name and inheritance rights would not be lost." Ruth marveled again at the compassionate kindness and care of the God of Israel for destitute widows and even for the dead.

At that point I don't think she dared to dream this provision would be for *her*, for she caught her breath and lifted her eyebrows, looking at me with a certain gleam in her eyes.

"Oh, goodness, child, I am much too old!" rolling my eyes in amusement at her girlish insinuation. "Besides, I'm beyond the age of childbearing." I could tell by her bewildered expression that she couldn't then comprehend my excitement, and that perhaps she considered him rather old.

That night as we sat at the dinner table opposite one another, she poured out the events of the day. She had "happened" upon this certain field. There had been some commotion when a somewhat older, middle-aged man (as she assessed him to be), came out to the fields to speak to the reapers. He seemed to be of some importance. As he passed each group of workers, he hailed them with a blessing that drifted on the wind: "The Lord be with you!"

And they called back, "The Lord bless you!" till the fields seemed to ring and the grain sway with blessing. It was evident that they all loved and respected him.

About mid-morning, while she was gleaning, Ruth noticed that he was looking her way while he spoke with one of the servants. Some discreet gestures indicated they were talking about her. Ruth had quickly looked down and turned her face away, becoming more diligently engrossed in the stalks of grain.

Then, she told me, he came directly over and spoke to her. "He called me, 'my daughter.'" Her gentle smile was accompanied with humble amazement. "He told me not to glean in any other fields but his and that I should stay close by his servant girls until the harvest was over." He even told her he had commanded the young men in his fields not to touch her. Apparently, he shared my fears regarding some of the young men in Israel who might take advantage of her. And he'd instructed her to drink from the water his men had drawn whenever she got thirsty. Blessed be Yahweh! Such specific answers to my prayers!

"What did you say?" My question compelled her onward.

"What could I say? He treated me so kindly." In her voice I could hear the awe that unmerited favor inspires. "I fell at his feet, bowing before him, and asked how it was that I had found such favor in his sight since I am a foreigner." So unassuming she was, so accepting of her unacceptable status.

"And?" I prompted. She was reticent to say more, but my eager eyes urged her to continue.

Boaz told her he had been given a full report of all her kindness to me since the death of her husband. Rather than treating her disdainfully for being a foreigner—and a Moabitess at that—Boaz recognized the emotional difficulty in leaving her father and mother and the land of her birth to come dwell among a people she had not known. He honored her for this. For him, her circumstances and her actions were but a window through which he could view her heart.

His compassion exposed my own heart. How self-absorbed I had been! I had not realized the extent of her sacrifice or the difficulty of leaving behind all that was familiar, even though I myself had experienced the same in going to her land. To me, it had seemed she was making the better choice, leaving behind what was false and degrading. Boaz helped me see her with new eyes, and my conscience smote my callous heart. I pondered long during the following weeks over his protective care. Before returning to Bethlehem, I had urged Ruth to go away from me. But Boaz had urged her not to go away.

Boaz believed so fully that Yahweh is a God of blessing and abundance who personally attends to our every attitude and action. With a clear understanding of the character of God, Boaz also modeled it. Knowing that nothing escapes God's notice and that no good thing will fail to receive His reward, Boaz pronounced a blessing over Ruth: "May Yahweh, the God under whose wings you have come to take refuge, repay you and fully reward your labor of love." Those words snagged on my heart. The God whom I had blamed, whose comfort I had rejected, in this same God Ruth had found a secure, protective resting place.

At lunch time, Boaz had sought her out again, offering her bread and dip and passing roasted grain to her. She saved some back to bring home to me. "Oh! That extra packet of food! I wondered where that had come from," I commented. Always she thought of me.

Going back out to the fields, she again saw Boaz talking with a group of his workers and gesturing in her direction. Gleaning throughout the afternoon, she became aware that the reapers were purposely pulling stalks of grain from their sheaves and dropping them in her pathway. "Ah! So that's how you came to glean so much in one day." I lifted my eyebrows as the answer to my earlier question

became quite clear. No scrounging a scoured field in search of some few straggling stalks! I advised her to remain in Boaz's fields, knowing she would be safe there.

As I looked into the face of my precious daughter-in-law, tears streamed down my cheeks. For the first time in many months, maybe even years, I sincerely thanked God for His goodness to us—to me. I was awed at the way God had answered my prayers. Yahweh had not forgotten us. Not ever. No, not even during those dark days when I felt like He had.

All through the barley harvest and on into the wheat harvest, Ruth continued to bring home abundant amounts of grain; we were well stocked for the coming winter. Occasionally she would also bring home another story of a conversation with Boaz and of his thoughtfulness toward her. Her eyes would glow with a shy, sweet gratitude as she recounted each incident.

While God was gently restoring me emotionally and spiritually, proving His love and care, I became convinced that a greater provision was foreshadowed in this physical supply. Our stores of grain were only a part and perhaps even just symbolic of something far greater, but I couldn't yet quite grasp all of it. I did begin to realize that I was just one woman in a long, rich heritage of those who had experienced the intimate, personal workings of God on our behalf.

I couldn't deny that God was faithfully charting our life journey. He was going before us, leading the way. Just as God had made a path through the Red Sea for our people those years ago, He was also opening the way before us. Just as He had provided for them in the wilderness, giving them bread from heaven and rivers of water from the rock, so He was providing for us.

Though all of life had seemed to give way and fall out from under us, God's Word never failed. Even when there were no good options, no way out of our deep needs, God was directing behind the scenes: guiding us, drawing us to Himself, giving us the strength we needed for each day, and teaching us to trust His love. His promises to care for us remained unchanged and forever faithful. God was working anew within the context of our present day lives.

During those days, one word kept replaying in my mind. It was the word I had used to compel Orpah and Ruth to return to their own land: that they might find rest in the homes of new husbands. Menuach—it is the rest found in security. Whereas I had been completely inadequate to provide a place of security for Ruth, God was more than adequate.

God's gracious law for young widows continuously pushed its way into my thoughts. While my hands spun the wool on my distaff into thread, my mind was busy spinning ideas into a plan. I felt somewhat like a young girl again myself! I broached the subject one night with Ruth at the close of harvest season. "Should I not try to find rest for you, my daughter, in the home of a new husband?" I asked her.

"But I am a Moabitess," she protested.

"Hush, my daughter. Did not even Boaz say that you have come to find refuge under the wings of the Almighty One of Israel? You belong to God—by faith. You are His, one of God's own people." And I reminded her that Boaz was a kinsman-redeemer to us. This time she blushed and knew exactly what I was talking about.

I knew that Boaz would be with his workers on the final night of threshing. Every year Boaz prepared a large feast to thank his reapers for their service, sharing with them the bounty God had so abundantly lavished on him. After the feasting, Boaz himself would spend the night at the threshing floor to protect the grain from theft or to cover the piles if it rained.

As I shared my plan with Ruth that night, she agreed in her gentle, submissive way to do everything I suggested. She bathed, put on lotions and perfume, and dressed in her most becoming clothes. *Oh, she does look and smell heavenly!* I thought as I viewed her through the eyes of love. Her whole being fairly radiated with a quiet joy and excitement.

At dusk, Ruth hurried through town, down to the field where the threshing floor was. As I had instructed, she hid herself and waited . . . till dark settled and everyone had gone home from the feasting. Still she waited until Boaz lay down to rest and she was certain he was sound asleep. Then very quietly she tiptoed to where he was, carefully drew the blanket off his feet, and lay down.

She told me her heart was pounding so hard she felt certain it would awaken Boaz! She could not sleep, as you can imagine, but lay resting at his feet hardly daring to breathe. Later, Boaz would tell us how he was startled awake that night—not by Ruth, but, as he believed, by the very hand of God.

Well, I certainly was unable to sleep! I lay on my mat, praying and waiting eagerly through that interminable night. With the first hint of morning light, before the sun was up, I heard her footsteps and called out, "Is that you, my daughter?" I jumped up to unlatch the door and saw instantly from the look on her face and the heavy bundle of grain wrapped in her shawl that all had gone well—even better than my imaginings!

Ruth recounted all that had transpired. The night had grown black as pitch when Boaz suddenly bolted up and realized someone was lying at his feet. "Who are you?" he whispered gruffly.

In a low tone she humbly replied, "I am Ruth, your maid-servant." Then, using the metaphor he had used of God, she asked him to take her under his wing, for he was our kinsman-redeemer.

Boaz responded with like humility, grateful and touched by her kindness at not being interested in the younger men. He again called

her "my daughter" and told her not to fear, promising to do all she requested. Then he added, "The whole town knows you are a woman of great strength and virtue." He told her to go back to sleep there at his feet until morning, for it would not have been safe for her to return home at that hour.

Before there was enough light to recognize anyone (so there would be no hint of indiscretion or opportunity for shameful gossip), Ruth got up to come home. But first Boaz had filled her shawl with barley—six times the amount she had gleaned on her first day! "You mustn't go *empty-handed* to your mother-in-law," he had told her. She relayed his words so innocently, amazed at his generosity. But I felt the point of the underlying message behind his well-chosen words. I had not come home empty, had I?

I hugged her and said, "Be still, my daughter. Rest. For he will not rest until he has settled this today." All the while God was teaching me to rest in His sovereign love and care.

I had been relying on my own efforts and on circumstances. If I weren't in such poverty, if only we'd had more time together, if I could just get past this, if . . . if . . . if. So I would try harder, plan better, analyze and scrutinize more—all vain attempts. Nothing changed. I could not undo the past or what was. Thoughts and words and prayers were hollow, devoid of meaning. My heart was broken, and an ever-ready fountain of tears threatened to spill over. There was nothing more I could do.

Looking back through our history at Job and Joseph and our ancestors in Egypt, I could see that God had been with them even during their times of deep despair. As I meditated on these things, God continued to press this lesson upon my heart: He is here. His presence surrounds us. He cares for us. It may seem to us that He is distant or detached from our needs, but He is not.

God understands grief and is Himself familiar with it. He feels our hurts along with us and is touched by them. He weeps with us in our sorrows. His Word proves these things. Though His deliverance may seem long in coming, God will meet our needs in His time. He sees the cares that weigh upon us, He hears our cries, He acknowledges our pain, and He is working to rescue us—that is what He told Moses. The eternal God has promised to be a refuge for us all our life long, through every trial.

If, like me, you have tried all you know to do and exhausted every option, just be still. He is God. Acknowledge this. And set your soul at rest, following not my example, but that of my dear daughter-in-law. Underneath you are the everlasting arms of God. Rest there. Fix your gaze on Him, and He will keep you in perfect peace.

Boaz indeed wasted no time that day in fulfilling his promise. After Ruth left the threshing floor, he went immediately to the city gate to await his opportunity. We had another relative who was closer kin to us than Boaz. Lo and behold, this man just happened to come through the city gate first thing that morning! Boaz detained him and gathered together the elders of the city.

Boaz was shrewd that day. This nearer relative was most eager to purchase our land; but when told he would have to acquire Ruth as well and be obligated to divide his inheritance with her progeny, he quickly retracted his commitment. According to our customs, as proof of the forfeiture of his rights to the land, our other relative removed one of his sandals and gave it to Boaz. All the elders in Bethlehem were witnesses of the transaction. To this day, Boaz has an extra sandal in his possession.

Right there at the city gate, the elders conferred a blessing upon Ruth: "May the Lord make her like Rachel and Leah." Ruth, an outcast? Oh, no! Far from it! Rather, she was elevated to the most exalted status alongside the first mothers of our nation.

And they gave to the household of Boaz the blessing of Perez. Perez? The events surrounding the conception of Perez weren't exactly the most stellar of circumstances, now were they? Oh . . . you don't remember his story? Well, if we got sidetracked wandering up the various tributaries of Israel's history, I would never finish my story! Suffice it to say that the conception of Perez was certainly a shameful mark in our nation's history—as all of us carry in our family lines. Nonetheless, Perez was, in fact, the patriarchal head of the tribe of Judah, a family line that otherwise would have been completely snuffed out due to sin and broken relationships.

However, God in His mercy reopened Judah's family line through Perez and his twin brother so that from the lineage of Perez, the ancient prophecy could be fulfilled: from the tribe of Judah, Messiah would come. As I considered the blessing of Perez, I realized his story bore a similar theme to our own. God had taken shame and brokenness, sin and all its curses, and used those very things to display the wonder of His redemptive power and grace.

Shortly thereafter, Boaz and Ruth were married. And it wasn't long before a baby was on the way. When he was born, Ruth laid him in my arms. I looked at her with tears welling up in my eyes. Her eyes also were misted with tears, and I read in them that she wanted me to understand that this provision of God was not just for her, but also for me: here was a son to carry on my husband's and my son's family line.

The women of Bethlehem, who had heard me complain so bitterly against God, now came not just to see the baby but also to bless Yahweh. They had had eyes to see what I up until then had not. The whole town had perceived Ruth's surpassing value long before I had. They were so right in what they said that day: I, who thought I'd come back empty and destitute, had really come back with a treasure of greater value than seven sons.

A few weeks later, I sat one day under a large sycamore tree, reflecting on my life. The spreading branches above reminded me of the far-reaching effects of all that had occurred. Not far from where I sat, a young seedling had sprouted from one of the dropped pods of the parent tree. In time it too would grow to be a great, expansive tree. Time, I mused—but it takes much more than time to heal the wounds of our hearts. God uses time just as He uses sun and rain. But it is only the mysterious, miraculous hand of God that can bring forth life out of death—even eternal life.

I marveled continuously at the ways and goodness of God, but not nearly so much as you are able to. Oh, what an advantage you all have that I did not have! You can look back on my life through the grid of the cross and the true Kinsman-Redeemer. If only I could have seen then what you can see now! God was allowing me the unparalleled privilege of playing an integral role in His redemptive plan. That was something I could not see until I had the eyes of eternity.

God had been in control all along. Ruth was a necessary piece in God's historic puzzle of redemption. He had entrusted our family with grief in order to bring this young Moabite woman to Himself and to Israel. The God who sees the end from the beginning had chosen Ruth to become the great-grandmother of King David. She and Boaz did indeed receive the blessing of Perez, entering the ancestral line of the Messiah. Through Ruth, God demonstrated throughout all time and eternity that His mercy and grace are available to all, regardless of our background, nationality, family line, or curses of sin. Boaz's redemption of Ruth was a significant link in the chain forged from God's desire to redeem the entire human race. How glorious is that?!

And not only that, but Boaz symbolizes what God Himself would eventually do for everyone of us—for you—by sending the promised Messiah, His own Beloved Son, whom He would bring forth from them in succeeding generations. He is the God who has noticed us in our need and stooped down to meet that need, even though every one of us is under the curse and poverty of sin and judgment. Like Boaz, God has gone out of His way to favor us with His blessing, taking upon Himself all that was necessary to remove the curse and open to us the abundance of His heart, His life, and His eternal home, a most secure resting place.

A young Moabite woman under the curse of God. An earthly kinsman-redeemer. And the heavenly Kinsman-Redeemer of all mankind.

In the process, God redeemed my life as well. Oh, if I could leave with you only one thought, it would be this: Trust the heart of God. In the midst of heart-shattering struggles, we have difficulty seeing how our set of circumstances could possibly be good. But to those who love God, that is exactly what He has promised: to weave everything in our lives together for good.

God's thoughts and ways are higher than ours. The clarity of our vision is restricted to the narrow window of the present moment. But He sees the whole panorama; His view is unrestricted. Our future is no mystery to Him. The sovereign, almighty God is both wise and good. He knows what He's doing, and He knows far better than we do what is best for us. His wisdom is never faulty. Though it may be difficult and painful at the time, His chastening is never unkind. It is never meant to harm us, but only to transform us. He is ever working to create in us the beautiful reflected image of His own likeness.

Why does He allow certain things in our lives? We don't always understand; His purposes may elude us. The severity of life often obscures our pathway with tears, blurring our vision of God. But He has never left us nor forsaken us. Only in looking back can we see that He has upheld us, carrying us in His arms all the way—from the womb to old age. Regard-less of how we may feel in the moment or how dim our view of His plans may be, we can still trust the intent of His heart.

Through the writings of Moses, God describes Himself as the One who carries us on eagle's wings. Like the mother bird who swoops down to catch her floundering young and carries them to their nest of safety, God lifts us up and hides us under the shadow of His sheltering wings. He is there—watching, guarding, guiding.

Trust Him, dear believer, for in Yahweh is everlasting strength. He is an ever-present help in our times of trouble. We all, even the youngest of us, have hurts and losses. I know that life here can be hard and even grievous, and that in the midst of it we often cannot see what God is really doing. But this I also know: God is sovereign, and His sovereignty, firmly rooted in His goodness and His wisdom, is a place of refuge. Like the outstretched protective wings of the cherubim who look down with wondering eyes over the mercy seat in the Holy of Holies, God's sovereignty overshadows us and is the best, the safest, and the most secure resting place for our souls.

God is at work. What He is doing in your life will be more than you could ever imagine. This life is so brief, and God has eternal purposes in view. Like me, you may not fully see His purposes or His reward until eternity. But you will see it. God is no man's debtor. Trust Him. Rest. Wait. His redemptive work is not done. Hope in God, for He has promised that those who hope in Him will never be ashamed or disappointed. I can testify to that. Now may the God of hope, who sent our great Kinsman-Redeemer, bless each one of you.

Beyond the Present Pain

Adapted from Genesis 37, 39-40

Introduction to
Beyond the Present Pain

Forgiveness: it's an area of life we all have to wrestle with. Some issues of forgiveness are harder to deal with than others. How can we respond with forgiveness when we've been betrayed, lied to, tromped on, or disregarded? How can we forgive when evil has purposely been perpetrated against us or when marriage covenants have been broken? I've had my own share of deep hurtful wounds, and I know from firsthand experience that forgiveness is not our natural response. In fact, I've come to believe that it is wholly a supernatural response, a work of God within.

When Jesus' disciples asked how many times we should forgive someone, His response stops us in our tracks with mouths hanging open in astonishment. Really? Seventy times seven? Like the disciples, we cry out, "Lord, increase our faith!" Obedience to that directive can only be supernatural, a work of magnificent proportions accomplished solely by the Holy Spirit within us.

When we've been wronged, the sovereignty of God is an anchor for our souls. It not only stabilizes us in the midst of persecution or during the circumstantial losses of life, but it also holds us fast in the face of injustice and wrong done against us, even when it's full-force evil. I cannot adequately extol the praises and the magnificent strength of the sovereignty of God. Oh, that all children of God would anchor their souls with this great historic truth. It will never let you down. There are no shifting shadows of unfaithfulness or of unwise decisions with this truth.

The sovereignty of God is the one truth we all must wrestle and come to terms with. We can either become bitter in the face of it, or we can find the greatest rest and comfort the world has ever known. By submitting to God's sovereignty, we will discover a peace that can never be taken from us no matter what is flung against us.

But the sovereignty of God can only become life-giving if we understand that it rests solidly on the goodness and wisdom of God. These things—the goodness of God and the wisdom of God—cannot be separated from the sovereignty of God. If they were, the sovereignty of God would be a monstrously fearful thing, a most dreadful reality. The sovereignty of God is eternally one with the loving wisdom of God, and in these conjoined truths we rest our souls.

Our difficulty with forgiveness, as our difficulty with any of life's trials, stems from our inability to see past the present pain. Being sinned against is a very real heartache. Our pain cries out for vindication. Forgiveness is not a laying down of justice, but a laying down of our pain to lay hold of the greater truth of grace. Without offenses, we could never learn this highest and best of all God's character qualities: Grace. Through offenses, He is giving us opportunities to be like Him. Could there be anything greater?

Choosing grace requires faith in the inseparable union of God's goodness and God's sovereignty. I pray that through the eyes of Joseph's wife you, like her, will come to see the wonder and power of forgiveness that can only rest on the foundation of the sovereignty of God.

Beyond the Present Pain

Likely you do not know me or remember my name. But the great God of wonders, the God who lives and speaks and sees, knows it and has recorded it in His Book for all eternity. I did not come to know the true God through great signs and miraculous deeds, but through the wonder of forgiveness forged out of trust in the sovereign hand of God. I am Asenath, the wife of Joseph, a man I'd never even met until the day we were married.

I well remember the wave of commotion caused in the capital the day a man completely unknown was led through the city streets in Pharaoh's second royal chariot. Pharaoh's head servants cleared the way before him, crying out, "Bow the knee! Bow the knee!" Overnight major changes were made in the political structuring of the kingdom of Egypt.

After horse and chariot had passed by, we lifted our faces out of the dust. Oh, how everyone began to chatter with curiosity and

queries! "Who is that man?" "Where did he come from?" "He doesn't look Egyptian." "Such a handsome man!" And then outlandish gossip began to fly!

As I hurried back to my father's temple to see what he knew of all this (for nothing happened in Egypt apart from the priests' knowledge and approval), I caught snatches of conversation: prisoner . . . slave . . . rape . . . dreams. What did it all mean? I couldn't imagine. Surely Father would know.

Upon my arrival at the temple, I quickly brushed the dust from my garments. I washed at the bronze laver as I entered the outer sanctuary. Quietly approaching my father's inner sanctum, I overheard him speaking with another. I paused to listen.

"Asenath." My father had heard me. "Come in, my daughter."

Pulling aside the curtained doorway, I recognized Pharaoh's chief advisor and nodded in homage to him. Then, going to my father's side, I took his hand and raised it to my forehead as I bowed in deferential respect.

"Pharaoh has sent for you, my daughter. You are to be married to the man Pharaoh has chosen to be second in command!"

I started and drew in my breath. "But, Father, do I even know this man?"

"Ah, it is a fitting position for you," he continued, ignoring my question. "Go now. Your mother will help you. And may the gods be with you," he added, smiling approvingly.

Growing up in my father's temple had taught me to obey without hesitation and to control any emotions embroiling within. But here before me was the biggest decision of my life, yet I had been dismissed with a wave of his hand. Nevertheless, I would play my role well and thus give my father honor.

After spending the next several days in a flurry of preparations, I was taken, along with an entourage of servants and belongings, to the royal palace. Keeping my head erect and my face serene, I entered Pharaoh's throne room to meet the man I was to marry. For a brief

moment, my eyes met his. I quickly lowered my gaze, but not without first noticing how strong and dignified he looked. A vague sense of familiarity haunted me, but I couldn't quite remember . . . Then it came to me and inwardly I caught my breath—the man in the chariot! I hazarded another glance; he was indeed uncommonly handsome.

That same day, we were married before Pharaoh, my father, and the entire court of Egypt. Standing motionless beside him, I wondered, "Who is this man? And what is his story?" Recalling the gossip from that morning over a week ago, it was all very intriguing and potentially dreadful. Now there were so many more questions than before. Yes, and fears.

As our marriage unfolded, so did his story—not immediately, mind you, but little by little. As events occurred, he would confide in me another portion of what he kept hidden deep within.

Right away he could tell I was apprehensive and wary. Joseph met this first challenge in our marriage with a disarming directness, laying out the entire episode between him and the wife of his master, Potiphar. He told of being bought by Potiphar, the captain of the guard. Oh, yes, I knew of Potiphar, a man of great wealth and power. I could hear the awe in Joseph's voice as he recounted the ways his God had prospered him and made him successful in all he put his hand to— so much so that Potiphar put him in charge of his entire household, leaving nothing outside his care.

Then, closing his eyes with a shudder, he carefully explained how Potiphar's wife began to tempt him. She would catch him off guard at odd moments, making up ways to be alone with him. "Because you're so handsome!" I teased with laughing eyes. He did not return my playfulness. Sin was no light matter to him; he did not view it as a joke to be laughed at.

With utter seriousness and absolute repugnancy, he said, "Day after day she spoke to me in these seducing ways. I reminded her of all her husband had entrusted to me. I appealed to her conscience, telling her I could not break my master's trust in this way, nor commit this great wickedness and sin against God."

Then came the day when he arrived at his master's house and sensed an ominous emptiness. Had she maneuvered to have all the other servants working outside that day? It certainly seemed like a set-up. This time, as he passed her with a curt nod, she took hold of him by his outer cloak and whispered temptingly, "Lie with me."

My eyes grew wide in amazement, and I noticed my breath quickening. But convictions set long before instinctively governed his immediate response. He rapidly, without hesitation, slipped out of his cloak and ran outside! The next thing he knew, she was screaming and calling the other servants in. Later he heard her story. She told how she had screamed when he'd tried to grab her!

I listened. Two stories: one of lustful intent to rape and one of innocent, impeccable integrity. When he finished, his eyes held mine with a clarity I'd never seen in anyone else before. He was not pleading for my acceptance of his story, nor groveling for my approval. He was simply waiting as I weighed the contrasting accounts. He knew what I was wrestling with.

"So that's why you were sent to prison?" I asked.

He nodded.

"Why didn't Potiphar kill you?"

He shrugged, offering no explanation or defense.

Beyond the Present Pain

"I believe you," I affirmed very deliberately. I was familiar with Potiphar's wife—a conniving, bewitching, catty woman. Taking his hands in mine I added, "I want to know this God of yours before whom you walk, a God who is worthy of your obedience even when no one is watching."

Ah! Let the people gossip! Of this I was now assured about him: he was a man of integrity. I'd never felt more secure in all my life. He had told me the truth apart from self-defense, manipulation, or pressure.

Then suddenly my mind reverted to the end of the story. I began to seethe inside. "But you went to prison!"

"Yes," he replied, his brief response indicating he'd rather not speak of it further.

Still, I ventured to ask, "What was it like in prison?"

He closed his eyes and his face contorted as he tried to rub out the furrows on his forehead. His voice low, he spoke in short, clipped phrases. "Hard. A dungeon . . . dark . . . dank. I was . . ." his breathing became more labored, "put in irons. Chained to the wall. Painful."

"I'm sorry," I whispered, almost wishing I'd not asked. Yet wanting to truly know him, I pressed on, hoping to extract more of the story. "How long were you there?"

"Oh, several years," he responded vaguely.

"Several years?! How horribly unfair! You must hate that woman!" I spat out my vehement outrage at the injustice.

"No, Asenath, I do not hate her." He spoke with a tone of finality. "I feel sorry for her, sorrier still for her husband. I think he knew the truth—which is probably why I'm still alive," and he gave a sorrowful half smile.

"I struggled with the injustice; I suppose everyone would. But ultimately, I had to wrestle it out with God. You see, Asenath, the God of heaven is not like the gods of Egypt. He is both sovereign and good." I looked mystified, so he continued, "He rules over all; nothing is outside His almighty will and command. And what He wills is always for our good, birthed out of His wisdom and His love for us. It took time, but," and he gave a short laugh, "I had no shortage of that. I was finally able to bend my will to God's and trust He knew what He was doing with my life even if I could not see it. Eventually I was able to settle my soul in the truth and affirm the belief that all of this had a purpose beyond my limited vision."

I marveled. False accusation, lies, maligning, injustice, pain . . . years spent in prison. But he harbored no bitterness. He expressed only grief for them. From the grid of my religious upbringing, I could not account for this. Forgiveness in the human heart is . . . well, it's not natural. No, it is supernatural, a miracle in the heart of man, a wonder of magnificent proportion. It is the work of God—a God I as yet knew very little about.

His family heritage remained a mystery to me. I just assumed he had come from an inauspicious slave background. What did that matter now?

One morning shortly before our first son was born, I recall watching him as he stood facing east, silently gazing past the front pillars of our home with a faraway look in his eyes. When he turned, he smiled at me in a contented, settled kind of way. But he said nothing.

At our son's birth, Joseph was deeply moved and profoundly joyous. I was quite bewildered when Joseph announced his name: Manasseh. It means, "making forgetful." Then he added, almost as if he were speaking to himself, "For God has made me forget all my toil and all my father's house."

The story didn't come out until a few days later. He arrived home early one afternoon, distant and preoccupied. As he took Manasseh from my arms and looked down at that little miracle of life, the same peaceful contentment I'd seen a few days before relaxed the lines of strain. He let out a faint sigh with a slight shake of his head.

"What is it?" I asked.

"The dreams," he replied. "What does it all mean?"

I was baffled by his question. "You know what they mean; you told Pharaoh yourself—seven years of plenty, seven years of famine."

"No, not those dreams." We sat down together and he began. For the first time, I learned of his family. I knew his origins were from the lands east of us, which was not uncommon for a slave. He told me he was one of twelve brothers born of his father's two wives, who were sisters, and their two servant girls. There had been much rivalry among the women, especially between the two sisters. Born in his father's older age, Joseph was the firstborn of the favored wife, who had been barren for many years. After Joseph had come one more brother, whose birth took the life of their mother. Their father, Jacob, had doted on Joseph, the eldest son of his beloved.

One afternoon his father had presented him with the most beautiful coat, very skillfully woven in many rich colors. "It was a symbol of my father's deep love for me, and also of his intent to give me the firstborn birthright, which meant a double portion of my father's inheritance," he explained. "However, my brothers, seeing the favoritism, were jealous and could never speak a kind word to me." In the midst of all that family turmoil, he had two very similar dreams.

"Just like Pharaoh!" I exclaimed.

"Well, yes, sort of." Joseph concurred. "But they weren't back to back in the same night as his were."

"What were they?" I asked, eager to draw it out of him.

In the first dream there were twelve sheaves, which he and his brothers were all binding in a field. Joseph's sheaf stood upright, while the other eleven sheaves all stood around his and bowed down.

I drew in my breath and covered a giggle, "I bet your brothers loved that dream! Not too much to interpret about that one, now was there? What was the second?" I asked all bright-eyed and eager.

In the second dream, the sun, moon, and eleven stars all came and bowed down to Joseph.

I made no attempt to muffle my laughter this time. "You didn't tell them that one, did you?"

"Well, I didn't act too wisely. I certainly did not comprehend the extent of their hatred, and I so wanted their approval." He paused, shaking his head at his youthful folly. "Yes, I told them, and my father overheard. Even he chided me reprovingly, 'Shall your mother and I and your eleven brothers all bow down to you?'"

"Your father didn't need an interpreter for that one either, did he?" I giggled.

"No. He felt his favoritism had gone to my head."

"Well, hadn't it?" I asked a bit reproachfully.

He frowned, his eyes cast down. A pained look came over his face. He was quiet for several minutes in self-examination. How many times had he asked himself the same question?

When he finally lifted his gaze, he looked deeply into my eyes with that same intent clearness. "I didn't make up those dreams, Asenath. They were not born out of my pride or of some desire to lord it over my brothers. God alone knows my heart, and He is the One who gave me those dreams. I am sure of that; they were too vivid. And they are as clear today as when I first had them."

"So, what brought all this up today?" I asked with a puzzled look on my face.

He took me back to the day he first rode through the dusty streets, standing in the back of Pharaoh's chariot. Seeing all the people bowing to the ground before him had suddenly brought those dreams flashing across his mind, so many years later.

"And today," Joseph continued, "no, not just today, but every day, I go to work overseeing the storehouses and reviewing the accountants' reports. Everywhere I go, people are bowing down to me."

"Then your dreams have been fulfilled!" I cried exultantly.

"No, they haven't," he murmured.

"OK. Go on," I encouraged, struggling to figure out his meaning.

"Everyone is bowing, but it's not my brothers and father and mother," he said in all seriousness.

This seemed rather arrogant to me—and maybe even a bit bitter, like a man who had everything the world could offer but refused to be content until he had all under his power. "What difference does it make?" I asked in a perturbed tone bordering on disrespect. Ah, but I had misjudged him again.

He waved me off, as if being misunderstood were a common thing for him. "Asenath, don't you understand? It's not the bowing down that I care about; it's the dreams. God's Word is true. He does not lie or tell half-truths. The dreams weren't about everyone bowing, but specifically about my brothers, father, and my mother's sister, who became like a mother to me after my mother died. That alone can fulfill the dreams."

I looked at him thoughtfully. He truly was not vindictive, desiring revenge upon his brothers; nor was he full of swaggering self-importance, seeking honor for himself. Rather, he felt intently zealous for the Name and Word of his God. "I'm sorry," I apologized, reprehending myself for adding my own character miscalculation to all the others. "So, what happened to your brothers and father and his wife?"

He was quiet. "I don't know," and he nearly broke down.

"What do you mean, you don't know?"

"I haven't seen or heard from them in over thirteen years." He let out a deep sigh as his eyes drifted toward the east.

"Why?" I questioned.

"They are in the land of Canaan. God has promised that land to my forefathers and their descendants."

I raised my eyebrows in questioning skepticism, "Oh? So they are still there?"

"I presume," he murmured.

Now I felt like I was trying to drag something out of him that was too painful for him to relive in words. "You don't have to tell me."

"I—I must." He looked at me with the pained expression of one who has long desired to unburden his soul in the refuge of another's trust.

He went on to tell me how his brothers had gone from bad to worse. They were unreliable, unfaithful men. Their father knew this, so he had sent Joseph to check up on them when they were herding their flocks in the north country. His father, too, had severely misjudged the depth of their hatred for Joseph, or he would never have sent him on that mission. As soon as Joseph came up to them, they mobbed him, tore off his beautiful coat, and threw him into a pit.

"Fortunately, the pit was dry, so I wasn't standing in muck and water up to my waist. Then they sat down to eat, arguing over how they would kill me and what they would tell father." His eyes still registered that look of vacant shock as he relayed the incident.

"Sat down to eat?" I shook my head in disbelief.

He ignored my remark; it was too painful. He continued the narrative, keeping an emotional distance from my reactions. "As it happened, my brothers saw some Midianite traders in the distance on their way to Egypt, loaded with goods. So my own brothers began to discuss the benefits of selling me as a slave over murdering me."

"How horrid! I can't believe they could be so cruel." I was indignant.

"I couldn't either," he agreed. He shuddered at the remembrance of how near he'd come to being murdered by his own brothers. Selling him as a slave served two purposes: his brothers would get some cash to divide among themselves while at the same time they would spare themselves the nasty unpleasantry of having blood on their hands.

My mind could hardly grasp this leap of understanding from who I had thought he was—a slave born of slaves in Egypt—to who he really was—the favored son of an aging wealthy man from the chosen people of God. I sat in stunned silence, my thoughts racing as I scrambled to put the pieces together.

I thought aloud, "So you were brought to Egypt, stripped of everything. Then Potiphar bought you because you looked like such a strong, sturdy youth. God blessed your work there and everything seemed to be getting better until Potiphar's wife fouled everything up and you landed in prison."

He nodded.

"And then . . ." I stopped. A piece of the puzzle was missing. "How did you wind up in Pharaoh's court? Why did he ask you to interpret his dreams? How did he even know you or that you could interpret dreams?"

Joseph went on to tell me of God's blessing even there in the prison, and of the jailer's favor. Recognizing his skill, his integrity, and the unusual blessing of God, the keeper of the prison put him in charge of the whole prison.

"Just like Potiphar did," I remarked, amazed. Regardless of the circumstances, however adverse, always there was favor. It was so evident that God was with him. Yet, if this was true, and if his God was sovereign over everything as Joseph believed, why had He allowed these things to happen to him? What kind of God was this? This was the biggest puzzle of all, and one not so easily put together.

Joseph continued, interrupting my mental struggle to sort it all out. "Some time later, Pharaoh's chief butler and baker met with Pharaoh's disapproval and were thrown into the same prison. They were put under my charge. I brought them their rations each day and tried to provide whatever meager comforts I could."

I smiled at him, this compassionate man of mine. His concern for others was born out of the womb of his own affliction.

"One morning, while attending them, I noticed that they both looked haggard and disconsolate," he continued. "Naturally, I asked the cause of their gloominess."

"Naturally," I nodded, "for you."

Not letting the compliment settle, he went on, "Interestingly enough, they had both had very vivid dreams in the night and didn't know what to make of them."

"Two dreams again!" I noted wonderingly. "How strange!"

He raised his eyebrows in agreement. "I asked them if they believed that God could interpret dreams and told them to tell their dreams to me." This time I marveled at the guilelessness of his remark, so untainted with personal pride, yet so confident that God communicated with him.

Beyond the Present Pain

"But," I interjected, "your own dreams had not—indeed, have not—come true! Didn't you ever doubt whether you really had heard from God? Or wonder if you could interpret dreams?"

He stared at nothing, silent for a moment. "I did have to wrestle that out with God, yes. But I had to look at the facts."

"Facts?" I questioned. "The facts seem to point to the conclusion that you were misled by your own imagination. What facts?"

"My forefathers. My great-grandfather Abraham had to wait until he was 100 years old before God fulfilled His promise to give him a son. But fulfill it He did! And my own father also had to wait. It was more than twenty years before God fulfilled His promise to him. My grandfather never did see the full realization of God's promise; it is still yet to come. But should we doubt God's Word simply because His timetable isn't what we thought it would be? No!" he spoke with great earnestness.

"Asenath," his tone softened, "you are seeing things only through the grid of circumstances. That is an all too common mistake," he chided gently. "God's Word in never wrong! Let God be true though every man be a liar. We cannot, we must not, doubt the Word of God no matter how strongly the circumstances seem to point the other way."

"That's what held you while in prison, isn't it?" I asked softly.

He pressed his point, "The fact that supersedes all other facts is the character of God: He cannot lie and He reveals His secrets, His plans, and His ways to the sons of men. You remember Pharaoh's dreams? Two dreams with the same interpretation, showing that the foretold events had been firmly established and that God would bring them about shortly."

"Yes, but your dreams certainly didn't happen 'shortly.'" I rolled my eyes.

"No, but they are firmly established." His voice carried a tone of finality.

"All right," I conceded. "So you based your faith not on your circumstances but on the clear revelation of God, 'the facts' as you call them."

"I think you're starting to get it," he grinned.

I shook my head and lifted my hands in frustration. "I just don't understand your God."

"I know, but you will," Joseph assured me.

I sighed, dropping my hands back into my lap in unwilling resignation. I lacked his confidence. "What were the dreams of Pharaoh's servants? Were they about you?"

"No," he shook his head.

Joseph related to me the dreams. The first was of three branches of grapes that budded and produced fruit. The butler had squeezed the grapes into Pharaoh's cup and then handed the cup to Pharaoh. The second was of three baskets of bread on the baker's head. Birds swooped down and ate the bread out of the baskets.

"Hmm. That's pretty cryptic," I said as I sought to puzzle out the meaning. "Kind of like Pharaoh's dreams with the fat cows, skinny cows; plump grain, shriveled grain. No wonder they didn't know what they meant. Why weren't your dreams cryptic like that? Sure could have spared you a lot of trouble!"

"Asenath, don't you see?" Joseph spoke so earnestly.

I shook my head, feeling hopelessly dull.

He tried to explain, "If they'd been able to interpret their own dreams, they wouldn't have needed me—or God. And if my brothers had NOT been able to interpret my dreams, I would not have had all my troubles. Without the troubles I never would have been in the right place to be where I am today. God *ordained* the troubles!" This was more than earnest; he was passionate. "God put me there so that He could give to those two men and to Pharaoh the answers they sought. He only used me to do it."

A small flicker of light glimmered in my mind, and I struggled to lay hold of it. But the baby cried. I rose to attend to him, and the flame snuffed out. By the time I returned, a servant had entered and courteously called my husband to other duties.

Throughout the rest of that day as I attended to Manasseh, I fought mentally to recapture that fleeting gleam of illumination but without success. How can one comprehend a God who claims to be only and always good yet ordains trouble, hardship, pain, even evil against His people?

Later that evening, I sought to continue our conversation. "Well, what was the meaning of those two dreams?"

Joseph explained that the three branches and the three baskets were both three days. In three days the butler would be restored to his position while the baker would be hung.

"Oh!" I gasped. "That must have been dreadful for the baker!"

"It was very difficult to relay the meaning of his dream," he admitted, "but it was the truth."

I still marveled at his confidence, considering his own dreams had so obviously been unfulfilled. "And what happened?" I asked.

"What do you think happened?" he asked in return, slightly incredulous at my question.

"They came true?" I replied hesitatingly.

"Of course," Joseph stated as an obvious matter of fact. "God's Word does not fail."

"So in three days all that happened?" I was still skeptical.

"Just as predicted," he nodded.

I jumped ahead of the story. "Then the butler must have told Pharaoh about you and gotten you out of prison!"

"Well," he paused, "in a manner of speaking, yes—two years later."

"Two years?!" I exclaimed. "You stayed in prison for two more years?"

Joseph took a deep breath before going on, "I asked the butler to please make mention of me before Pharaoh when he was restored. I told him that I'd been stolen from my native land, that I'd done nothing to deserve the dungeon. But evidently he forgot."

"How could he? The ungrateful . . ." I began to spew out my boiling anger, but Joseph put his finger to my lips. I looked at him in an almost desperate silence, searching his face. "You say that without malice. How? Why?"

"The sovereignty of God," he firmly asserted without hesitation. And again more earnestly, his eyes piercing deeply into mine as if to make me understand, "The sovereignty of God, Asenath. His ways, His plans, His timing are not ours. He is wise. He sees what we cannot. We must trust Him." That momentary flame of illumination flickered again, yet still eluded me.

"Then what happened?" I whispered.

"Pharaoh had his two dreams. No one could interpret them. Hearing of Pharaoh's dilemma, the butler remembered me. I was summoned. They cleaned me up, and here I am." He held his arms out and smiled, his face so utterly free of even a hint of rancor.

I walked into his outstretched arms and looked up at him with deep respect and amazement. "And that was the day I first saw you." The baby stirred. "And you named him Manasseh, because God has made you forget the hardship of your past. Has He?"

"I am content. God has been good to me," Joseph quietly affirmed. It still seemed a rather dubious goodness to me.

A couple years later another son was born. This one Joseph named Ephraim, which means "fruitful." Looking down at his new-born son, my husband said, "God has caused me to be fruitful in the land of my affliction."

For my husband, my country would always be the land of his affliction, yet it was also the land where he was greatly blessed. I knew he felt rich with a fullness not dependent on circumstances or on what others did or didn't do. God had not been taken by surprise or caught off guard by the sins of man.

The fullness God gives is not destroyed by pain and struggle. Rather, it is solely dependent on a sovereign God who honors those who honor Him. God's blessing does not require ignoring or forgetting the heartaches of life, nor is it dependent on continual ease and pleasure.

I began to redefine my understanding of both forgetful and fruitful. Forgetful was not the lack of memory. Neither did the blessing of fruitfulness necessitate the absence of affliction. With Joseph's God, forgetfulness and remembrance, fruitfulness and affliction could peacefully co-exist and even merge . . . into fullness.

The years of plenty ended. The famine came as God had revealed. Was I surprised? Well, seven years is a long time. We had grown so accustomed to bounty; surely that prediction would not affect us. How could such abundance suddenly vaporize? But Joseph never doubted the famine would come. He pursued his mission with unwavering determination and a looming sense of urgency as the seven years of plenty came to an end.

The rains ceased; the land grew parched. The contrast was stark and undeniable. In one city after another, Joseph began to open the warehouses as the lean months passed into years.

"Asenath! Asenath!" My husband's voice was urgent as he flung back the door and rushed into the house.

I ran to him, "Joseph, what is it?" He was trembling all over, weak with emotion and excitement. I pulled him over to the couch and put both hands on his shoulders to steady him. Again I asked, "What? What is it?"

He searched my face and was breathing heavily. "In the will of the Lord, those Midianite traders came by that day. In the will of the Lord, my brothers sold me to them. In the will of the Lord, I went to prison. I knew that, but I couldn't understand. Finally I'm beginning to see!"

"In the will of the Lord?" I objected as the fog of incomprehension settled over me again. "I still don't see how can you say that."

110

"They've come!" The way he said it filled me with a vague and uncertain dread.

"Who has come?" I returned an alarmed look, seeking to quell the panic rising within. I had no idea to whom he was referring.

Again his eyes darted across my face, searching to see if I would comprehend the import of this moment. I nodded slightly, waiting.

"My brothers."

I involuntarily sucked in my breath, "Your brothers?" It had been so long since he'd told me about them. As the memory of his dreams flashed through my mind, my grip on his shoulders tightened. "And they bowed to you," I stated with absolute certainty.

In wonderment he slowly nodded a silent "yes."

"Let God be true though every man a liar," I quoted his words.

He smiled into my eyes that warm handsome smile of his. Then he stood and drew me to him. "So your dreams have finally come true," I whispered.

"No, not quite." A small sigh escaped from him, lightly brushing my cheek.

I drew back and looked at him questioningly, "What do you mean?"

"In my dreams all my brothers were there. Today there were only ten."

Suddenly dozens of questions flooded into my mind and tumbled out one on top of the other. "What did they say? Had they come for food? Which brother was missing? Do you know why? Where is your father? Is he still living?"

He paced the room amused. "You sound a bit like me," he grinned. "Only I asked with more decorum as befits a person of dignity!" There was playful reproof in his tone. "They didn't recognize me."

I gasped again. "They didn't?! What did they do when you told them who you were?"

"I didn't tell them." Instantly he turned steely serious. I waited, my breath coming rapidly as a shiver ran down my spine. "I had them thrown in prison."

I misread a note of finality in his voice and my blood ran cold. This was not like him. It was a side I'd not seen before and it frightened me.

He saw my recoiling. "It's not as you think." He paused, considering how to explain his motives. "I have to know first if they've had a change of heart. I cannot commit myself to them until I know. True forgiveness, Asenath, cannot be given carelessly, as if the offense never happened. I needed time to think. I accused them of being spies, attempting to gather information to overthrow our country."

As he continued to accuse them, they defended themselves by giving him the information he was seeking. Is my husband not an exceptionally wise man?!

"They told me they were all sons of one man, and," his voice was tinged with a note of sarcasm, "that they were honest men." He gave a rueful half smile. His words hung in the air as he stared at nothing, reflecting on their dishonest ways, which had caused the whole chain of treachery and excruciatingly painful events. It seemed a whole life-time away now. "They called themselves 'my servants.'" The irony of it was written all over his face, a controlled contortion like a dam on the verge of breaking.

"When I accused them again, they told me they were twelve brothers, the sons of one man. It was Benjamin who did not come. They said he had stayed behind with their father. So, yes, my father is still alive!" His eyes glistened with tears as he struggled for control. "I suppose Father is afraid to part with him for any reason, especially in their company." A slight fierceness entered his voice. "And I," here his voice broke, "I, they said, was no more." Now the tears streamed down his face. "That's why my father never sent for me, never searched for me, never tried to rescue me. I'd thought as much. He's been told I'm dead. Honest men! They have continued the lie for twenty-two years!" He dropped his face in his hands and shook with sobs.

"Perhaps they think you did die." I sought to soften his thoughts.

"Perhaps. But neither did any one of them attempt to find out. This is why I must try to determine what is really in their hearts," Joseph concluded.

"But how?" I questioned.

He looked at me blankly, helplessly. "I don't know." His voice suddenly sounded tired and worn. How I wanted to help, but I didn't know how. I wanted to fix it all, but I couldn't.

He kept his brothers in prison for three days, during which time he was deep in thought and prayer. The days seemed interminable. My heart grew ever more anxious, but I held my peace. Are we not, in the waiting periods, so given to manipulation, to wanting quick fixes? But I learned through my husband's example to cease my striving and wait on God: He alone is able. For Joseph would be the first to tell you as he told Pharaoh the day he interpreted his dreams: "It is not in me. God will give the answers that bring peace."

Beyond the Present Pain

I wondered what his brothers were going through. Joseph did not go to see them but had his servants keep a faithful watch. I saw the change on his face the day he released them from prison. A focused peace and quiet determination came over him. He told them he would retain only one of them. The rest were to go back with food to bring relief from the famine for their families. Then, they were to return with their youngest brother to verify their words. Otherwise, they could no longer buy grain and their brother would remain in prison.

"But what if they treat Benjamin as cruelly as they did you? Are you not afraid for him?" I asked.

"Their lives depend upon him now—because of the famine," he responded.

A light began to dawn in my understanding: God had orchestrated all these details to reach into and expose the inner, hidden places of their hearts. Oh, the depths of the riches both of the wisdom and knowledge of God! How unsearchable are His judgments and His ways past finding out!

As Joseph's plan began to unfold, I again found comfort and security in him: first in his integrity and now in his wisdom. He was no longer the impetuous youth seeking approval or affirmation from his brothers. Here was a fully mature man, secure in his God, testing the hearts of men.

"Reuben was the one who saved my life; I found that out today." He rather carelessly tossed out this bit of information.

I snatched upon it as he knew I would, my eyes growing wide with interest and curiosity, "How did you find that out?"

"I spoke always through an interpreter," he began rather flatly as though he were reading the numbers on a granary report. "When I gave them my stipulation, they began to argue among themselves—that part hasn't changed!" His tone shifted, rising slightly before settling again. "They, of course, didn't know I could understand them. They admitted their guilt to one another, remembering my anguish of soul when I pleaded with them to let me go back to father. They actually described it quite well." He stopped, trembling with the remembrance. "They believe that the trouble they've run into here is a direct punishment from God for what they did to me."

"Well, I guess in a way, they're right about that! If they only knew . . ." How stupefied they would be if they had even a hint of the truth.

Joseph continued his narrative. "Reuben angrily reminded them how they refused to listen to him when he told them 'not to sin against the boy.' Then he added, 'Behold, now his blood is required of us.'"

"So they do think you are dead," I observed.

"Apparently. They've lived the lie for so long, they've come to believe it themselves. Perhaps that's easier for them to believe than the possibilities of the alternative." He sighed heavily. "I had to leave the room; I couldn't keep from crying." He covered his eyes, reliving the pain even as he recounted it to me. "Simeon is now in prison. They watched me bind him. It wasn't easy. I've sent the others off. Now we will wait again—who knows how long."

We learned that God's plans for us most often involve waiting—not idly, mind you—but waiting with the active effort of self-control, which trust requires. When our waiting is based on trust, we purposely choose to place ourselves moment by moment in the sovereign hand of God by faith in His Word.

Joseph did not like having Simeon in prison. The emotional strain weighed on him. We waited day after day with mixed emotions, not knowing what would happen if and when they did come. Yet each day we couldn't keep from hoping that this would be the day they would appear. As we waited, we prepared our hearts. Choosing to release all bitterness, anger, and desire for revenge, we held forgiveness in readiness. When would they return? All we had to cling to was the certainty of what God had revealed in the dreams.

An interminably long time passed. We learned later it was because Joseph's father was unwilling to let Benjamin go, and his brothers knew it was pointless to return without him.

Suddenly, without warning, late one morning our house was swarming with servants. "The master is having eleven important guests for dinner, Mistress," one told me in answer to my query. Eleven guests! My heart pounded. Could it be? I caught a glimpse of them as they approached the house. All bearded men, definitely not Egyptian. It had to be them.

I stayed out of sight, straining to listen and watching from behind some curtains. They thought they were being framed because of the money my husband had generously put in their sacks on their first trip—Joseph had wanted the food to be his gift to his family.

Beyond the Present Pain

I saw them approach the head steward and make a respectful and groveling appeal. I almost felt sorry for them. They were nervous and very fearful.

Our dignified steward took his cues from my husband. How graciously he spoke to them, sounding almost angelic. "Peace be with you. Do not be afraid. Your God and the God of your father has given you the treasure in your sacks. I received your payment for the grain," he calmly reassured them.

Simeon was then brought out to them. I could not understand their words but saw the general relief and rejoicing at their reuniting. They were all ushered into the house and given water to wash. I watched as they whispered among themselves and made ready an elaborate presentation of spices, nuts, honey, and lotions. Quite an abundant array, I thought, for a time of famine. It revealed the extremity of their anxiety.

When Joseph finally arrived, he only had time to pause briefly as he passed me. I felt his apprehension and saw in his eyes the longing of years. He silently mouthed the name, "Benjamin." I nodded, tears welling up in both of our eyes. Then he left.

I watched him as he entered the banquet hall, his bearing completely recovered. He stood erect, dignified and confident, in total command. At his appearance, the men hastened to offer their gifts. I caught my breath and put my hand to my mouth as I saw enacted before me dream number one: all eleven brothers bowed low to the ground before (though they did not yet know) their despised brother.

Again came the words emblazoned on my mind, "Let God be true though every man a liar."

I was nervous; my hands were clammy. How would it all play out? Through an interpreter, I heard my husband ask with an authoritative tone about their father. He was well, they said as they again prostrated themselves before him. "Oh, thank You, Lord God," I breathed a silent prayer. I knew without doubt now that the other dream would just as surely take place.

They arose. Still not giving himself away, Joseph asked through his interpreter, "Is this the younger brother of whom you spoke?" In a tender tone of benediction, he looked full at Benjamin and said in our Egyptian dialect, "God be gracious to you, my son." Even as he spoke those words, his controlled demeanor crumbled. He hastened out of the room, leaving the brothers looking at one another in perplexed consternation. I ran to our chamber and knelt beside my husband, putting my arms around him as he wept.

When he regained his composure, he washed his face in cold water to remove any traces of crying. Then he reentered the hall. Restraining his emotions, he ordered the meal to be served. There were Egyptian dignitaries seated at one table, my husband at the head table, and his brothers at yet another table, for Egyptians do not eat with foreigners.

The steward seated each brother as my husband had specified. Oh, it was comical to see their expressions of astonishment as he placed them one by one in birth order! You could tell it gave them an eerie feeling. It was too uncanny.

Beyond the Present Pain

Joseph purposely showed favoritism to Benjamin by ordering the servants to serve him five times as much as the others so he could ascertain his brothers' reactions. The other brothers thumped him on the back, joked about it, and were jovial all through the dinner.

"It did appear that they have changed!" I commented to Joseph that evening. But it still wasn't quite enough. Their response could have been just one of relief. To be more certain, Joseph designed one last test. He instructed his steward to again place each man's money in the top of his sack and to put his personal silver cup in Benjamin's sack.

Hoping to prevent them from fabricating some story as they'd done in the past, Joseph would lead his brothers to believe he used this cup to divine messages from the gods in order to foretell the future and read people's minds. By singling Benjamin out as the one who would have to pay for this "crime," Joseph would be able to ascertain whether his brothers would carelessly go on without their youngest brother or return to protect him.

My husband was restless all evening and his sleep fitful. The brothers were given rooms in our home to sleep for the night. The next morning they left in high spirits, relieved to be on their way back with Benjamin and Simeon. Joseph gave them just enough time to get out of the city before sending his steward after them, with specific instructions regarding what to say and how to search each sack from the oldest to the youngest, to heighten the tension. You could tell the steward was relishing his role in this drama, and he played it well!

Joseph, however, remained home that morning, pensive. An hour passed. Was the steward's life in danger? Time seemed to stand still.

Then suddenly, in a riot of emotion and action, the climax rushed upon us. A servant ran in, bowing. "They're back, sir," he said panting. The steward ushered them in. They were completely distraught. They had torn their clothes. They flung themselves onto the ground before him. Now I truly did feel sorry for them.

Joseph again spoke harshly to them, accusing them. This time, amazingly, they made no defense, no justification, even though, in truth, of this they were innocent. They saw this turn of events as God's hand against them for the evil they had done those many years ago. Finally, they were willing to be souls bared, mouths stopped.

Judah, the one who had spoken up to persuade the others to sell Joseph those many years ago, again became the spokesperson. This time he offered all of them as Joseph's slaves.

But Joseph wisely and methodically put them to the final test. With the pronouncement of a just judge, he declared, "Far be it from me that I should do so. The man in whose hand the cup was found, he alone shall be my slave. And as for the rest of you, go up in peace to your father."

The set trap had now sprung. I could hardly breathe. I watched as Judah drew near to Joseph's throne of power and heard his pleading, contrite speech while on his knees before him. Still speaking through an interpreter, he told the whole story that had transpired during the long wait between their first and second visits to Egypt. He spoke of his father's sorrow over Joseph's death and unwittingly revealed the lie they had foisted upon their father: that a wild animal had torn Joseph in pieces that day he'd gone to check on his brothers.

With utmost tenderness and earnestness, he told how his father's life was now bound up entirely in the life of this youngest son. There was not even a hint of self-centered jealousy, but rather a sacrificial willingness to lay down his own life to rescue Benjamin. That hardened heart of stone had been transformed into a heart of flesh. Only God can effect such miracles. Judah appealed to Joseph, fearing that the sorrow of losing this second beloved son would be the final breaking of his father's heart and lead to his death.

As Judah's speech continued, I could see the flexing of Joseph's facial muscles as he struggled to maintain his composure. At the conclusion, Joseph unexpectedly cried out to all his servants standing by, "Make everyone go out from me!"

The brothers were taken aback and frightened, not under-standing his words but seeing their effect. Shrinking away, they huddled together watching fearfully as the hall was cleared but for them. Alone, they stood before Joseph as he stared at the ground breathing heavily.

Then Joseph looked at his brothers and, knowing their change of heart, the dam broke. Twenty-two years of pent up emotions flooded out, and he wept loudly and uncontrollably. The brothers stood motionless in shock; they had no clue what to make of this. Finally, they heard him speak for the first time in their own language as he managed to say through broken sobs, "I am Joseph! Does my father yet live?"

The brothers' shock turned to dismay and dread. But Joseph spoke compassionately to them and asked them to please come near to him. They did so, but only in mechanical obeisance. Again Joseph repeated, "I am Joseph, your brother, whom you sold into Egypt."

He was quick to understand the emotional responses this would elicit. As he had often done with me, he addressed it directly, "Don't be grieved or angry with yourselves for selling me here. God sent me before you to preserve your lives." Whereas they had wanted to destroy him, he embraced his purpose in the sovereign will of God: to save their lives! I wanted to run to him right then and throw my arms around him in loving gratitude for the man he was.

Three more times he reiterated to them, "God sent me before you to save lives. It was not you who sent me here, but God. Tell my father, 'God has made me lord of all Egypt.'" Long before today, this truth had settled his heart: God is sovereign. That was the bedrock foundation of his life. God had known the end from the beginning, and His plans and purposes cannot be thwarted. God is the great Initiator of ALL things. He can be trusted—regardless of the circumstances or how those circumstances come to us.

He told them there would still be five more years of famine. Then, wonder of wonders, far from any thoughts of bitterness or vengeance, Joseph invited them to bring their wives and children down to Egypt, promising that he would provide for them. As they stood in stunned silence before him trying to take it all in, he had to repeat his identity again, urging them, "Look at me." His hands motioned to his face. "Your eyes and the eyes of my brother Benjamin see that it is the mouth of your own brother that is speaking to you." When we have chosen to believe a lie for so long, sometimes our minds cannot accept reality even when it is placed plainly right before us.

The rest of the morning was emotionally charged. Joseph and Benjamin wept together as they embraced one another. All twelve brothers sat together sharing their lives, filling in the gap of twenty-two years. It was beautiful—something only God could do.

Was it worth the pain? Was it worth the wait? Yes. Unequivocally, yes. Look at all the good that came out of it! Would we have willed any of that to be different? God had a work to do in all of their hearts, including my husband's—and mine. It had to be this way, so God could save them—and me.

126

Beyond the Present Pain

Pharaoh heard about Joseph's reunion with his brothers and was delighted. Servants were sent scurrying to prepare donkeys laden with provisions and carts with horses in order to bring all their families with their father down to Egypt to live out the famine. As Joseph sent them away this time, he warned them with brotherly affection not to become troubled along the way. He was so insightful about human nature. How easily our fears and doubts and guilt come back upon us!

That night he lay beside me thoroughly drained but so full of happy gratitude to God. It wouldn't be long before he would see his father again. The past was truly behind him. And the future? Safe in the arms of God.

The reunion with his father, Jacob, was the most joyous spectacle I have ever witnessed. We had the privilege of sharing seventeen more years with him. He loved our sons dearly and delighted in their growth to manhood. Through them, Jacob received great pleasure in reliving the years of Joseph's boyhood as well as sharing in some of the years he had missed in Joseph's life.

As Jacob's death drew near, he blessed our two sons as his own, crossing his arms to place his right hand on the head of the younger and his left hand on the head of the older. Joseph started to protest but then restrained himself as he realized his father was taking himself back nearly one hundred years. By putting the younger son

over the older, Jacob was recalling how he, the younger twin, had received the firstborn blessing, the seal of God's covenant promise with him.

Then Jacob called for all his sons and prophesied over each one of them. For Joseph was reserved the longest and most beautiful blessing of all. There was no glossing over the facts of the bitter grief and hatred Joseph had endured. But Jacob also triumphantly acknowledged Joseph's enduring strength through it all—strength derived from the Mighty God, the Shepherd and Rock of Israel.

Beyond the Present Pain

At that moment the elusive flame of illumination blazed into full light. Now I understood that the God who ordains the trouble is able to multiply and expand one's latter end so much more than the beginning that, as a result, the former griefs are not remembered—at least, not in the same way. The trials God plans—yes, *plans*—for us are not meant to harm us. He is the God who promises that when we pass through the fire, we will not be burned; and through deep waters, they will not overflow us.

When Jacob had finished, he drew his feet into the bed and breathed his last. My husband flung himself on his father, kissed his face, and wept and wept. I think they were tears of gratitude as much or more than those of sorrow. A lengthy Egyptian funeral was commemorated for his father. Afterward, Jacob was buried in Canaan, the land of promise, as he had requested.

When they all returned again to Egypt, Joseph's brothers became anxious. Now that their father was dead, they thought perhaps Joseph's anger toward them would be aroused, and in hatred he would seek revenge. Too afraid to come themselves, they sent messengers, appealing to him in the name of their father not to count against them their trespasses and all the evil they had done to him. The messenger added the brothers' own confession of guilt and remorse, pleading for his forgiveness.

When he heard this, Joseph wept—for two reasons: For the first time his brothers fully and personally admitted their guilt to him. It had been thirty-nine years in coming. And also, their fear demonstrated that they still misunderstood. Had he not proven by his actions, by his care and provision, that he had indeed forgiven them, that they were brothers?

Later, his brothers also presented themselves to him, bowing low before him once again and offering themselves as his servants in fear for their lives. I don't think I've ever seen such compassion and grace flow from a mere mortal man. Joseph was indeed God-like.

"Do not be afraid." He spoke with pity and a tinge of sadness, for they still did not understand. "Am I in the place of God?" he asked. Oh, if only he could help them understand as he had helped me. "As for you, you meant evil against me." As always he was clear and direct, uncompromising with truth. He did not try to hide or diminish the evil that had been done, yet he was full of tenderness. "But God meant it for good, to bring about what is now, the saving of many lives," he affirmed, attempting to press this truth upon their hearts.

With these words he revealed the depth and strength of all that had anchored him. He let God be God: Sovereign Initiator of every detail of his life, Planner and Orchestrator of history, Judge and Avenger, Vindicator and Defender. Joseph, the offended, sought to comfort his offenders. "I will provide for you and your little ones," he pledged. A miracle of true forgiveness.

Can a person be put through the pain of the sins of others and come away unscarred? Is it possible? My husband's life proclaims a triumphant, "Yes!"

What about you? Have you been sinned against? Are you struggling to forgive someone? Don't allow someone else's sin, even if it's against you, to lead you to doubt the trustworthiness and goodness of God. Nor let the sins of others waylay you in your own sinful quagmire of bitterness or tempt you to throw away your own integrity. It matters! Stand strong. Stay on course. Keep trusting that God has your life and all its details in His hands.

Remember this: forgiveness does not flow naturally from us. It must be a work of God in our lives. It is hard won out of wrestling with God, until our hearts rest unresistingly yielded to His sovereignty, affirming His goodness in the very thing that has caused us pain. Out of this settled peace with God is borne the fruit of forgiveness.

Will you believe that the trial you are in, that grief you are bearing, the sin that has caused you so much sorrow is God's *plan* for you? Will you trust that the hurt you've endured will not harm you? Will you allow life's offenses to be the tool used by God to shape His grace within you? In what other way are we able to learn grace, this greatest and highest of all God's gifts? For the very definition of grace—extending undeserved, unearned forgiveness and love to those who have wronged us—requires offense. In all of life, in all your circumstances, embrace the sovereignty of an always good, always wise God, which enables us to forgive even the most painful of offenses.

We may not clearly see and understand God's purposes. No, maybe not until eternity. But will you trust Him? He means it for good. Let God be true though every man a liar: He is good and His purposes—for you—cannot be thwarted. Let God be God.

Rebecca has been a student of the Bible for many years and loves to encourage believers with the life-giving truths of God's Word. Over the years, Rebecca and her husband have been involved in various ministries, including church planting and discipleship in the Philippines, pastoring a growing church in Texas, serving in Christian camps in Alaska and Washington, and assisting at a family retreat center.

On the home front, she homeschooled their seven children over a span of thirty-two years. As the mother of seven and grandmother of a growing troupe of grandchildren, Rebecca is a strong advocate of family discipleship. She has taught homeschool classes, women's retreats, and home Bible studies.

Writer, speaker, singer, and harpist, Rebecca shares the astounding life-giving, life-changing truths the Holy Spirit has taught her through the Word of God, presenting the wonder of an all-wise, all-good sovereign God. Primarily she would like to be known as a fellow pilgrim on the compelling and sometimes arduous journey of trust in a loving, faithful God.

For blogs on homeschooling, Titus 2 mentoring, prayer, and Christian life and Bible study themes, see her website:
www.reservoirofgrace.com

Rebecca can be contacted through the above web address for speaking engagements or dramatic presentations for homeschool, women's ministry, or special church events.

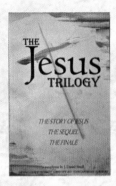

The full story of Jesus, from His birth to His Kingdom reign as Lord of lords and King of kings, is told in a fresh way through this chronological compilation of all four Gospels, combined with the book of Acts and the book of The Revelation.

Written by J. Daniel Small, *The Jesus Trilogy* is not only a skillful paraphrase, it is a new way of organizing the essentials of the complete story of Jesus, making this rendering unique.

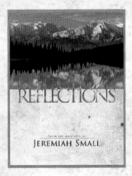

Reflections presents a collection of hymns and journal meditations from the emails of Jeremiah Small during his time as a high school teacher in the Kurdish region of northern Iraq. This book includes a brief biography of his short but full life.